STILL NOT INTO YOU

CHARLOTTE BYRD

CHARLOTTE BYRD
dangerously addictive

Copyright © 2020 by Charlotte Byrd, LLC.

All rights reserved.

Proofreaders:

Julie Deaton, Deaton Author Services, https://www.facebook.com/jdproofs/

Renee Waring, Guardian Proofreading Services, https://www.facebook.com/GuardianProofreadingServices

Savanah Cotton, Cotton's Incision Editing, https://www.facebook.com/Cottons-Incision-Editing-512917856115256/

Cover Design: Charlotte Byrd

No part of this book may be reproduced in any form or by any electronic or mechanical means, including information storage and retrieval systems, without written permission from the author, except for the use of brief quotations in a book review.

This book is a word of fiction. Names, characters, places, and incidents are either products of the author's imagination or are used fictitiously. Any resemblance to actual persons, living or dead, events, or locales is entirely coincidental. The author acknowledges the trademarked status and trademark owners of various products referenced in this work of fiction, which have been used without permission. The publication/use of these trademarks is not authorized, associated with, or sponsored by the trademark owners.

Visit my website at www.charlotte-byrd.com

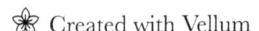

❦ Created with Vellum

ABOUT STILL NOT INTO YOU DUET

You were once the man that I hated, but I forgave you for what you did.

Now, it's your turn to forgive me.

No, I didn't cheat on you, not even close. But I made a huge mistake, the kind that few relationships survive.

What now? Where do we go from here?

It was the stupidest thing I've ever done, and it changed everything.

Will you find it in your heart to forgive me?

Or is this the end of us?

** STILL NOT INTO YOU is the second book of bestselling author Charlotte Byrd's enemies-to-lovers DUET that will leave you head spinning.

It was previously published as One Weekend but the text has been substantially expanded and revised.

What readers are saying about Charlotte Byrd's Books:

"This book/series is addictive! Super hot and steamy, intense with twists and turns in the plot that you just won't see coming…" ★★★★★

"One-sitting read!" ★★★★★

"How on earth did I survive that? **My mind is blown,** my hearts beating out of my chest and I'm on this cliff, shaking like a leaf in a windstorm waiting to do that all over again with the conclusion to one of the best reasons to get out of work and get lost for a while." ★★★★★

"This series is just so **intense and delicious.** The stunning twists, raw emotions and nerve wracking tension just keep increasing as each book in this enticing series unfolds. I am so invested in Nicholas and Olivia. These characters really worm their way into your heart, while also totally consuming your

mind. The gripping story quickly captivates and pulls you back into this couple's world. Do try to be prepared for the cliffhanger and the wait for the sixth and final book in this amazing series."
★★★★★

PRAISE FOR CHARLOTTE BYRD

"BEST AUTHOR YET! Charlotte has done it again! There is a reason she is an amazing author and she continues to prove it! I was definitely not disappointed in this series!!" ★★★★★

"LOVE!!! I loved this book and the whole series!!! I just wish it didn't have to end. I am definitely a fan for life!!! ★★★★★

"Extremely captivating, sexy, steamy, intriguing, and intense!" ★★★★★

"Addictive and impossible to put down."
★★★★★

"What a magnificent story from the 1st book through book 6 it never slowed down always surprising the reader in one way or the other. Nicholas and Olive's paths crossed in a most unorthodox way and that's how their story begins it's exhilarating with that nail biting suspense that keeps you riding on the edge the whole series. You'll love it!" ★★★★★

"What is Love Worth. This is a great epic ending to

this series. Nicholas and Olive have a deep connection and the mystery surrounding the deaths of the people he is accused of murdering is to be read. Olive is one strong woman with deep convictions. The twists, angst, confusion is all put together to make this worthwhile read."
★★★★★

"Fast-paced romantic suspense filled with twists and turns, danger, betrayal, and so much more."
★★★★★

"Decadent, delicious, & dangerously addictive!" - Amazon Review ★★★★★

"Titillation so masterfully woven, no reader can resist its pull. A MUST-BUY!" - Bobbi Koe, Amazon Review ★★★★★

"Captivating!" - Crystal Jones, Amazon Review ★★★★★

"Sexy, secretive, pulsating chemistry…" - Mrs. K, Amazon Reviewer ★★★★★

"Charlotte Byrd is a brilliant writer. I've read loads and I've laughed and cried. She writes a balanced book with brilliant characters. Well done!" -Amazon Review ★★★★★

"Hot, steamy, and a great storyline." - Christine Reese ★★★★★

"My oh my....Charlotte has made me a fan for life." - JJ, Amazon Reviewer ★★★★★

"Wow. Just wow. Charlotte Byrd leaves me speechless and humble… It definitely kept me on the edge of my seat. Once you pick it up, you won't put it down." - Amazon Review ★★★★★

" Intrigue, lust, and great characters...what more could you ask for?!" - Dragonfly Lady ★★★★★

WANT TO BE THE FIRST TO KNOW ABOUT MY UPCOMING SALES, NEW RELEASES AND EXCLUSIVE GIVEAWAYS?

Sign up for my newsletter: https://www.subscribepage.com/byrdVIPList

Join my Facebook Group: https://www.facebook.com/groups/276340079439433/

Bonus Points: Follow me on BookBub and Goodreads!

ABOUT CHARLOTTE BYRD

Charlotte Byrd is the bestselling author of romantic suspense novels. She has sold over 600,000 books and has been translated into five languages.

She lives near Palm Springs, California with her husband, son, and a toy Australian Shepherd who hates water. Charlotte is addicted to books and Netflix and she loves hot weather and crystal blue water.

Write her here:
charlotte@charlotte-byrd.com
Check out her books here:
www.charlotte-byrd.com
Connect with her here:
www.facebook.com/charlottebyrdbooks
www.instagram.com/charlottebyrdbooks
www.twitter.com/byrdauthor

Want to hear about new releases, free books and get exclusive giveaways?

Sign up for my newsletter!

YOU ARE INVITED!
Want to hear about new releases, free books and get exclusive giveaways?
Join my Facebook Group!

Sign up for my newsletter: https://www.subscribepage.com/byrdVIPList

Join my Facebook Group: https://www.facebook.com/groups/276340079439433/

Bonus Points: Follow me on BookBub and Goodreads!

facebook.com/charlottebyrdbooks
twitter.com/byrdauthor
instagram.com/charlottebyrdbooks
bookbub.com/profile/charlotte-byrd

ALSO BY CHARLOTTE BYRD

All books are available at ALL major retailers! If you can't find it, please email me at charlotte@charlotte-byrd.com

Wedlocked Trilogy
Dangerous Engagement
Lethal Wedding
Fatal Wedding

Not into you Duet
Not into you
Still not into you

Tell me Series
Tell Me to Stop
Tell Me to Go
Tell Me to Stay
Tell Me to Run

Tell Me to Fight
Tell Me to Lie

Tangled Series
Tangled up in Ice
Tangled up in Pain
Tangled up in Lace
Tangled up in Hate
Tangled up in Love

Black Series
Black Edge
Black Rules
Black Bounds
Black Contract
Black Limit

Lavish Trilogy
Lavish Lies
Lavish Betrayal
Lavish Obsession

Standalone Novels
Debt
Offer
Unknown
Dressing Mr. Dalton

1

We are still more than an hour and a half away from home. I try to quench the anticipation building in the pit of my stomach with something fun to think about. I ask him about his family. I haven't heard anything about them for a long time. As we start to talk and laugh, I discover that there's so much that we hadn't talked about. It all suddenly floods in.

For instance, Hudson thinks that his little brother, Cayden, is gay. Gay and doesn't know it.

"How can he not know it?" I ask. "He's fifteen! Maybe he's just not gay."

"Well, in that case, he's in denial or something. I'm pretty certain that he is."

"Maybe he's just afraid to come out?" I ask.

"Why would he be? He knows that my parents won't care. They'll probably be happy," he says.

"It takes a while to be comfortable in your own skin," I say. "You have to be patient. I mean, I still can't come out to most people about being a writer."

We don't just talk about serious things. We also talk about funny, heartfelt things. Like last Christmas.

"Do you remember when you chased me around the house for my candy cane?" I ask.

"No!" he says imperatively. "It wasn't yours. You got it as a gift, yes, but you hate candy canes. And by the way, who the hell hates candy canes anyway? They're peppermint and sugar. I know for a fact that you love peppermint tea."

"That's not at all the same thing." I shake my head, smiling. "What's important is that that was my candy cane and you just expected me to give it over."

"Because you weren't going to eat it."

"You didn't know that."

"Oh, yes, I did." He nods furiously. "I found that stash of candy canes in your closet from the year before. You didn't eat one. You just kept them all away from people who actually like them. You greedy, greedy girl!"

We crack up laughing. I laugh so hard, my eyes tear up. When he catches his breath, Hudson turns to me.

"I've missed you, Alice," he says as we pull up to

our building. He's planning on returning the rental car tomorrow. After parking, we head straight up to our dorm.

"I've missed you, too," I say in the elevator.

A flood of emotions starts to sweep through my body the higher we climb. If I don't do something, tears will flow out of my eyes and I won't be able to stop them. I lean up to Hudson and kiss him.

In the middle of that passionate and explosive kiss, as he tears at my clothes and messes up my hair, I suddenly realize that I don't need an apology from him over the breakup. I don't want to think for a second about what this all means. I don't even want to know if I want him back. I just want to be with him.

We kiss furiously until the elevator beeps and the doors open. We stumble out, almost forgetting our bags inside. At the last minute, Hudson shoves his hand in between the doors to keep it from leaving. Reluctantly, the elevator opens.

When we get to our dorm, I head straight to the bathroom.

"Okay, I'm going to hop in the shower and I'll meet you in your room?" I say.

"Unless you want me to join you?" He winks.

I roll my eyes and shake my head.

When I get out of the shower, I reapply my makeup just a bit. I brush my hair, flip it over to give it some life, and leave it damp. I look in the mirror. Is this really happening?

"Just breathe," I say to myself. Suddenly, I wish that I had one of those tattoos on my wrist that says 'just breathe.' I've made fun of those on many occasions. I mean, when do you really forget to breathe? At this point, I could use one. A visual reminder to relax. Take a break. Breathe in and out.

My heart beats so hard, it feels like it's going to jump out of my chest. I knock on his door. No one answers. I knock harder. When he doesn't answer again, I push it open.

Hudson's sitting on his bed with his laptop. He barely looks up. He has a despondent look on his face. When he looks up at me, he doesn't look at me so much as through me. Somewhere far away.

"What's wrong?" I ask.

He shakes his head but just a little bit. It looks so much like a nod, but different. I wait for him to speak. A minute passes. It feels like a century.

"I...I...lost the money," he finally says. His voice shakes.

"What money?"

"The money I invested with Dylan's guy," he says slowly. There's a difficulty in each word, it's as if to say it, he has to move a car singlehandedly from one side of the street to another.

"Oh my God, I'm so sorry." I wrap my arms

around him. He doesn't push me away. Just continues to sit here. Lost in a world that I can't reach.

"I lost $15,000," he whispers, burying his head in his hands. "How could I be so stupid?"

"I'm so, so sorry." I embrace him.

I don't know what to do to make him feel better. I wish there was something, but I feel utterly helpless. *Just be here for him,* I say to myself. *Just sit here and listen.*

"It was going so well. My $5,000 investment became $10,000. I was going to take it out, but then I didn't. I put it all back in, Alice," he says.

Whilst at first, words didn't come at all, now they're practically tumbling out of him. "Why did I do that?" he asks. "I'm so stupid."

"No, you're not," I whisper.

"I made another $5,000 and then…then it all disappeared."

"How?" I ask.

He takes a deep breath and lets it out and then says, "The stock plummeted after the CFO of the pharmaceutical company was arrested for insider trading."

We sit in silence for a long time. I don't know what to say and Hudson has nothing else to say. Eventually, and with a great deal of effort, I turn off the light and take the laptop from his lap. I pull the covers over him and give him a kiss on the cheek.

"Where are you going?" he whispers.

"I thought I'd give you some time to rest," I say.
"Can you stay? Please?"

I climb into bed with him. Hudson wraps his arms around me. He presses himself against me. We spoon for some time. Minutes tick away. Sometime later, I turn to face him. I think that he's asleep, but he's wide awake. Still staring out in the distance.

"You should get some sleep," I say. "Things will be better in the morning."

Hudson looks at me. He disentangles his hand from the covers and brushes his index finger along my bottom lip. His fingertip feels soft like silk. Slowly, he pulls himself closer to me. I feel his breath on my lips. Our lips touch.

His lips are effervescent. He parts my lips with his tongue. It feels familiar and strange at the same time. As we kiss, our bodies morph into one. I can no longer tell where he begins and I end.

Suddenly, his kisses become more forceful. He presses his whole body into mine. Every last inch of it is hard and strong. He climbs on top of me and kisses me harder. So hard that it borders on painful. I try to keep up. I push back into him. He rises a little above me. I'm surprised at my own strength.

We make out well into the night. It doesn't go further than that. We don't rip our clothes off. We simply make out. Like teenagers. Because, mainly, we still are. I don't want to lie. It's not like thoughts of pulling off his clothes don't strike me, but I don't

Still not into you

initiate. He doesn't either. At this moment, this is enough. This is more than enough. Sometime later, after we're both worn out, we fall asleep in each other's arms.

2

It's 3:37 a.m. when I sneak out of bed to get something to drink. As I pour myself a cup of milk, Dylan comes in and flips on the lights. He startles me. I shield them as best as I can, but the bright lights still sting my eyes.

"Hey, I'm so sorry. Didn't know you were in here," he says.

Dylan's dressed in a suit. The one he wears exclusively to clubs.

"Shit, Alice, I'm not having a good day," Dylan says.

"Neither is Hudson," I say.

He looks away. Pours himself a cup of water. "Oh, he heard? I was going to tell him in the morning."

"He lost $15,000, Dylan," I say, crossing my arms.

"Oh, shit, I didn't know it was that much. I thought he'd only invested five."

"No, he invested his gains back into it."

"Ah, well, that's what happens." Dylan shrugs.

"Is that all you're going to say?" I ask. "That's all his savings. He lost everything."

I'm so angry, I want to punch him.

"Hey, if it's any consolation, I lost twenty grand. Just about." He shrugs.

"Yeah, but he doesn't have a rich dad to bail him out," I say. "You can still afford to go party all night. He can't."

Dylan shrugs. He doesn't look like he cares much.

"How could you let this happen?" I try again.

I have to make him understand. I know I shouldn't be doing this at three in the morning, after I didn't get much sleep and he has been out all night, but I can't stop myself.

"Hey, listen, it was an investment. He knew what he was getting into."

"But it was your guy!"

"So what? That guy made him $10,000! Would you be here yelling at me if he had pulled out?"

"No, but he didn't, did he? He lost all his money!"

"I don't want to hear this shit, Alice," Dylan says. "I lost a lot of money, too. Hudson's a big boy."

Still not into you

"He's right," Hudson says, coming out of his room. "He's right, Alice. I knew about the risks."

"But don't you think Dylan should've warned you—"

"No," Hudson cuts me off. "It's fine, really. It's not Dylan's fault."

"It just sucks," I say. "You lost so much money. I just wish I could help."

"I know, but you can't. No one can. It's fine," he says.

"No, it's not." I shake my head and open the door to my room.

I leave Hudson and Dylan alone. If he's not mad at him, why should I be? I rub my eyes. Juliet turns around in bed. She's engulfed in her comforter and I can barely see her face. Only her eyes.

"Sorry to wake you," I whisper and close the door behind myself to block the light from the kitchen.

"It's okay," she says. Her voice is raspy and uneven. "Dylan and I broke up."

"Oh, I'm so sorry," I say, changing into my pjs.

"It's okay," she sighs. "He's back with Peyton. Again. He's obsessed with Peyton."

Though I can't see very well, I can tell that her eyes are puffy. She has been crying.

"Hey, weren't you supposed to be away for the weekend?" she asks.

I fill her in on the details. Simon. Hudson.

Hudson and I making out. Hudson losing his money. Wow, this has been a ridiculously long day. Just going over it in a few sentences tires me out.

She listens quietly, taking it all in. Doesn't comment. I'm grateful for that. I couldn't deal with a snarky remark right now without getting too emotional about it.

"So, how are you?" I ask. She doesn't respond right away.

"Eh, fine. You live and learn, I guess," she says.

I've always wondered what that expression meant. It's as if it's a way to just write off a huge part of life and not deal with it. It seems enlightening and worldly, but it sounds like an excuse. Like a statement that someone makes when they don't want to make a statement at all.

"So, what did you learn?" I ask.

She's just trying to cope with this. I shouldn't be putting her on the spot like that. I know that and I hate myself for doing it anyway.

"What did I learn?" Juliet asks like she's trying to buy time. "That I shouldn't go out with assholes."

We both laugh.

"That's going to be a tough thing in this city," I joke.

I DON'T SEE Hudson until that afternoon. In the morning, he goes for a run and then I go out for brunch with Juliet. She's still distraught over Dylan, but trying to put on as brave of a face as possible. That afternoon, she goes out to a matinée show of *A Streetcar Named Desire* with some of her acting friends. I'm invited, too, but opt to stay home. The drizzle that started that morning has morphed into a full-blown rainstorm and I have a hard time braving the streets of New York in this kind of weather.

The good thing about not going to the cabin for the weekend, one of many, is that I actually have time to edit my paper due on Monday. I was in a rush to finish it before the trip and now, for the first time this semester, I'm actually done two days before it's due. The feeling is quite exhilarating, I can't lie. There's this heavy feeling of dread that lifts off me. I don't have a dark cloud hanging around my head about a paper that I should be writing but I'm not. It feels so good, actually, that I decide to try to finish other papers early as well. It might be a pipe dream, but it's good to have dreams, right?

There's a knock on my door just as I finish reading the last sentence of my paper.

"Come in," I say. I click save and close my laptop.

When I turn around in my chair, I see Hudson standing awkwardly in the doorway, unsure about coming in.

"Oh, hey, how are you?" I ask.

"Okay, I guess." He hangs his head. "I went for a run this morning. To clear my head."

"And?" I ask hopefully.

"I'm still finding it difficult to get over the fact that I lost fifteen grand, but I guess I'm feeling better than last night."

I nod and ask him to come in. We both sit down on my bed together.

"On the bright side," I say. "At least, you had fifteen grand to lose. I mean, that's something, right?"

That was my bad attempt at a joke. It backfires. He looks crushed. I feel like a massive idiot for even saying something like that. Something so insensitive.

"I'm sorry," I say. Too little, too late.

"No, that's true, I guess. Just a little too soon, I think."

I nod, grateful that he doesn't take it personally.

"So, I mainly wanted to come here and talk to you about Dylan," he says.

"Dylan?"

"I don't want you to talk to him about this anymore. You shouldn't have lectured him about this."

"I was just trying to help you," I say defensively.

"I know, but I don't need it." He shakes his head. "It's not Dylan's fault. I don't think he scammed me. He lost a lot of money, too."

"I know, but—" I start to say.

"No buts, Alice," he cuts me off.

Still not into you

I feel this incessant need to make Hudson understand that I was coming from a good place. I don't know why. I don't think for a second that he might already know that.

"It was an investment. That's what happens to bad investments," he adds. His voice is forceful, certain. I look up at him. There are flames of anger in his eyes.

"What's wrong? Why are you mad?" I ask.

"Why? Because you are butting into my business. Do you know how embarrassing that is?"

"I was just trying to help."

"Alice, I don't need you to–" he yells. Then stops short at the end of the sentence. He doesn't finish it. It's like he's afraid of finishing it.

"You don't need me," I say. "I get it."

I get off the bed. I don't want to see his face. Yesterday was like a dream. Not necessarily a bad dream, just a dream. It doesn't feel real. I walk over to the window and look out at the pouring rain outside. The whole city is crying.

"That's not what I meant," Hudson says.

I wait for him to put his arm around me, but he doesn't. He simply walks to the door and leaves.

3

I don't know whether it's from lack of sleep and general exhaustion, but I suddenly break down sobbing. This is the first time I've cried like this since our actual breakup. I feel like I've been holding it all in for so long and now it's finally out.

"No, I can't do this anymore," I whisper to myself through the tears.

An hour passes. My tears dry up. I open a textbook to try to get some studying in before finals next week. A knock at the door breaks my concentration.

"Can I come in?" Hudson asks.

"No." I shake my head. "I'm busy."

He sits down next to me anyway. Takes my hand. I try to push him away, but he doesn't let me. I look into his eyes. There's a hint of hope and a whole lot of regret in them.

Hudson leans toward me and takes away my books. He drops everything on the floor. I let him.

He leans closer to me. Presses his soft lips onto mine. Breathes me in. As we kiss, his hands start to slide down my body. Eventually, they find where my sweater ends. He finds his way underneath. With one swift motion, I'm on my back and he's lying halfway across me. This feels so good. I can't stop him even if I wanted to. He traces the curves of my hips and pulls on the strings of my pajama pants. He pulls my pants down a bit, until my hipbones are exposed. Then he pulls away from my mouth and kisses my hips. One. Then another. His fingers tease my belly button. I sigh, close my eyes, and let it all happen. Hudson's always been an expert with his hands and lips.

My body rises and falls with each kiss. Slowly, I pull off my shirt and take off his. He unbuckles his pants. I drop my bra to the floor. He wiggles out of his pants. Helps me out of mine.

"I've missed this, Alice," he says in my ear.

I love the way he says my name. I've missed this, too. Lying naked next to him with our bodies intertwined, I feel at home. Like I've never belonged with anyone else. His breath matches mine. Our hearts beating at the same pace.

He climbs on top of me, draping me with his whole body. I'm in a cocoon. I'm safe. I grab onto his shoulders for leverage. His muscles are hard and strong, but the skin is as soft as silk. We move in unison. We moan in unison. When it comes, I look into his eyes and see stars.

"Well, that was good," Hudson says, wrapping his arms around my shoulders and snuggling next to me. "Thank you."

"No, thank *you*," I whisper.

When we were together, we started a quirky tradition of thanking each other after sex, if we were both left satisfied. I'd completely forgotten about it until he said those words. They make me smile. We lie in bed for sometime as darkness starts to fall. It's not even 5 p.m., but twilight comes quickly, especially on rainy and cloudy days. I know that Juliet will be getting back soon, so I start to get dressed.

"I've missed you, Alice," Hudson says, propping up his head with his hand.

"I've missed you, too," I say, tossing him his underwear and jeans. "Juliet will be home soon."

When we are both dressed, I remake the bed.

"I want you back, Alice," Hudson says.

I've been wanting to hear those words a long time. Since the summer. Now that I'm actually hearing them, I don't feel the way I had thought I would. Making love was wonderful, but I don't want him back. We shared a good moment, but maybe that is all it's supposed to be.

"No, I can't Hudson." I turn to him.

This is not what he had expected to hear. I see the fire and hope in his eyes disappear. Disappointment sets in.

"What do you mean?" he asks.

"Hudson, this was nice. Really nice."

"Nice? Are you crazy? This was amazing."

"Okay, yes, it was." I give him that. "But I don't think it's right for us to get back together. Not now."

"Not now?" he asks. I see that I've given him hope. That's not what I meant to do.

"Not ever," I say definitively.

"Why?" Hudson asks. He puts his arms around me, but I push him away.

I don't know why. It doesn't feel right. I try to figure out why.

"You're in a tough spot now, Hudson. I get it. I'll be there for you as a friend. A really, really good friend. But you just want to get together because you're lonely or anxious about the future. You don't have to be, I'm here for you, but I can't be your girlfriend again just because you're going through a tough time."

Disappointed, he walks away but stops at the door.

"I don't want to be with you because of the money. It has nothing to do with that. You asked me why I came to the cabin. It was because I was worried about you with Simon, but that wasn't all of it. I didn't come up because Tea and I broke up. I came to see you because I missed you and I want you back. I made a mistake, Alice."

I nod. Take a breath. I don't go to him.

"Alice, I was a real jerk. I shouldn't have ever broken up with you. There was nothing wrong with us. I just did it because I didn't think that we should be so serious in college. I thought we were too happy. Like it couldn't possibly last because we were too happy. I was so stupid, Alice. Childish. I wanted to date other people. When it came right to it, I couldn't. Not really."

"Thank you," I say after a while. "I understand now."

I am grateful for the explanation. I didn't know it, but I've waited for the truth about why we broke up for a long time. Now, it is out there. I have closure.

He's waiting for me to come to him. To forgive him and say that I love him and that everything's going to be okay. His arms are to his sides. He's shown me all of his cards. I know that he's telling the truth, but something's holding me back.

"I love you, Alice," he says. It's his last attempt.

"I love you, too," I say quietly. "I'm sorry. But I just can't."

Tears cloud my eyes. A large one breaks free and rolls down my cheek. My throat aches from sorrow.

4

It's finals week. Where did the time go? Halloween and Thanksgiving were a blur. I went home for Thanksgiving, but I hardly remember any of it. Thankfully, my finals are spread out and aren't stacked up like Dylan's and Hudson's. I don't have any double final days and have at least a day to study for the next one. It could be worse, of course, but it could also be better. I look at Juliet. She's practicing breathing for her breathing class. I wish I had a breathing test instead of three final papers.

I haven't talked to Hudson for a couple days except for a brief, "Hello, how are you?" The more time goes by, the stronger I feel that my decision is the right one. I can't even begin to express how nice it was to be with him again, but life isn't just about what happens in bed. It's more than that and despite what he says, I'm not entirely sure this isn't some sort of freaking out moment for him. Maybe he took the breakup with Tea harder than he'd thought. Maybe he's upset about losing all that money. Either way, he's not in the right state of mind to make a decision as big as this one. I'm sure he's just confused. I'm pretty sure. Then that voice in the back of my head stirs up. I don't want to hear it but it's there. What if he's right? What if he just wants to be with me and all those other things just happened to happen at the same time?

American Lit is my first final of the year. Many people finish early, but I write practically every thought I have in the little blue notebook. I write until my hand cramps, un-cramps, and cramps again. I go through two notebooks, but finally get every last bit of knowledge that I have about *The Invisible Man, To Kill a Mockingbird,* and *Catcher in the Rye* onto paper. Tea and I are the last people to finish. I follow her out of the classroom. She looks tired and worn out. It's the first day of finals. I haven't looked at myself in the mirror, but I know that she looks a lot better than I do. She's at least wearing jeans and a proper sweater. Whilst I'm dressed in the same sweats that I've slept in.

"How do you think that went?" I ask.

"As best as it could've." She gives me a weak smile.

"Yeah, I feel the same way," I commiserate with her.

Still not into you

"Hey, listen, I heard about you and Hudson. Are you okay?" I ask.

"I'm fine." She nods. "He just wasn't all there. I don't think we were ever right for each other."

"Are you sure?" I ask. I'm trying to find out what happened. As if more details are going to give me a better understanding about my own decision.

"Yeah." She shrugs. "He never really wanted to be with me. He said that he wasn't ready for a relationship. I should've listened to him. He was telling the truth. I just couldn't see it."

"I'm sorry," I say. It's the only thing I can say.

"It's okay. We weren't meant to be. You know what's funny? After it was over, after I broke up with him, I thought I would feel terrible, but I didn't. I felt relieved. So, I guess that was the right decision."

"Yeah, seems like it."

We say our goodbyes. Give each other a warm hug.

"Have a wonderful Christmas," she says.

"You, too," I say. "And don't forget to let me read your book when you're done. I know it's going to be amazing."

"You'll be the first." Tea smiles.

WHEN I GET BACK to my room, all I want to do is plop down on the bed and listen to an unhealthy amount of Adele. Someone on our floor is blasting

Christmas music, and though I hate to admit it, it puts me in the holiday spirit. I only have two more finals. Then I'm done. First semester of college finished. I can't wait to be free.

I grab a can of soda out of the refrigerator before heading to my room. I'm about to walk in when something on the dry erase board outside on our door catches my attention.

Can we erase everything and start all over again? – Hudson

I read the words carefully, to make sure that I'm not dreaming.

I feel him come out of his room and stop right behind me.

"Hudson, what are you doing?" I ask. "I thought we'd gone over this."

"I know we did, but the thing is that I don't think you believe me. I think you think that I want you back because of Tea or losing all that money. I don't. I want you back because I'm an idiot. I just realized that I never really stopped loving you and I never will."

I clutch my bag. He doesn't shift his weight from one foot to another, the way he usually does when he's nervous or uncomfortable. Instead, Hudson stands up straight, his eyes fixed on mine. At this moment, not even an earthquake can break him away from me.

"I love you, too, Hudson."

"So, what is it? Do you not believe me?"

Still not into you

"No, I do believe you."

"So, why can't we be together?" he asks.

"Because I'm afraid." I take a deep breath. "I'm afraid of going through all this again, Hudson. Getting over you was one of the hardest things I've ever done. And, honestly, I don't think I can do it again. I'm sorry."

I go into my room and close the door. I want to be with him more than anything. I want him to take me into his arms, tell me that everything's going to be okay. I want to believe him, but I now know that this requires a big leap of faith. The kind of leap of faith that I'm not sure I'm capable of. Not now. There's something else. There's a sneaking suspicion in the back of my mind that this burning desire to be with me might blow over after finals. I hope I'm wrong. I just can't know. Either way, I can't think about this anymore. I have two more finals to worry about.

5

Two sleepless days later, I'm finally done with the semester. When I come back home, I find Juliet tossing all of her notebooks and papers from the semester into the trash.

"You're getting rid of everything already?" I ask.

"ASAP. I'm done!"

"I don't know if I can do that," I say. I've never been one to throw away all of my notebooks, not even in high school where this was practically the ritual every June.

"What if you need to review something later on?" I ask.

"Why would I need to do that?" she asks. "Finals are over!"

I don't have a good answer. I want my academic life from this semester out of sight as well, but I opt to drop all the papers into the bottom drawer of my desk.

"We're all going out later to get drunk," she says. "You in?"

"Of course," I say. "My flight home isn't until later tonight."

"Awesome. I'm going home tomorrow. I think that's when Dylan's leaving, too. Not sure about Hudson."

I nod. "Oh, hey, so how are things with you and Dylan?"

"They're good, actually." She smiles. "It was just a fling. Being friends is best."

"So, is he back together with Peyton?"

"Oh, I have no idea." She laughs. "I thought he was, but then he said that he wasn't. Those two are addicted to each other. He told me that they've broken up and got back together like ten times! So much drama."

"I never thought I'd hear that from you." I laugh.

"Oh, I like drama. On stage. On screen. A little bit in my life. But his level of drama is out of control. No, not for me."

We crack up laughing. As different as Juliet and I are, I know that I'm going to miss her over break.

"So, you never told me, what are you doing for next semester?"

"What do you mean?"

Still not into you

"Weren't you planning on moving out? Not living with your ex again?" she asks.

"Oh, that. No, I'm planning on staying. We're in a good place now," I say. "Honestly, I completely forgot to even file the paperwork."

"Well, that's good. For me, at least." Juliet smiles. "'Cause I kinda like you as a roommate."

"Oh, really? Well, I kinda like you as a roommate, too."

LATER THAT AFTERNOON, while we wait for Dylan to come back from his last final, I decide to pack. As I pull the suitcases out of the closet, all the clothes from the top shelf fall on me.

"Great. Just great," I mutter and start sifting through them.

I need some warm clothes, but not that many. Definitely don't need the really warm sweaters or the snow boots. Unless, of course, I go skiing, which is a possibility. Shit. I'm going to have to lug all of this crap back home. I start tossing all of my favorite clothes into the bag. I should be rolling them like my dad showed me, to maximize room, but I'm not really in the mood to organize. What will fit will fit and that's it. I have more clothes at home, clothes that I didn't wear for four months. Might be a nice change.

As I rummage through the closet, I work up

quite a sweat. I decide to open the window to let in some fresh air. I don't see the box of thank-you cards on the windowsill and they go flying out.

"Shit! Oh my God!" I scream, but it's too late. They are already halfway down the building. Since they weren't thank-you cards that I ever planned on mailing out, I didn't bother with the envelopes. They open up mid-flight and take on air. Most take their time and fall at a leisurely pace, letting the wind take them on an adventure.

"What's wrong?" I hear someone yell back up to me. It's Hudson. He's standing at the bottom of the building.

"My cards!" I scream. "They're going everywhere!"

"I'll get them!" he yells.

"I'll be right down!" I yell back, pulling on my Uggs and grabbing my coat.

With just my luck, the elevator stops at practically every single floor. People are done with finals. They're happily chatting away. On two occasions, I have to tell them that I'm in a hurry as they hold the elevator open saying their goodbyes. I should've taken the stairs, but it's too late now. I tap my foot anxiously. My cards are probably all over Manhattan now. Ten minutes later, I finally get onto Broadway. Hudson stands at the corner with a thick stack of cards, reading one. I look around the street. Don't see a single one.

"Hey, that's private!" I say loudly, so that he can

Still not into you

hear me over the sound of afternoon traffic. An ambulance rushes by, deafening me to the point where I can't even hear my own thoughts.

Hudson doesn't look up. It's like he can't hear me.

"That's private," I say, walking up to him. He looks up.

"It's addressed to me," he says.

From the cover, I can tell that he's reading the last card I wrote. Why did it have to be that one? I wish more than anything that he were reading any other card.

"It's still private. I didn't mean for you to read it. I was never going to send it."

"Dear Hudson." He ignores me and starts reading. I try to get the card out of his hand, but he lifts it above his head, continues to read out loud. "Dear Hudson, I'm just writing to say thank you. Thank you for coming back into my life as a friend. Thank you for saying all those things you said. I've been waiting for you to say them for a very long time. I love you, too. I'm going to love you for as long as I live. You were the best first boyfriend that a girl could dream of. I don't think I'm ever going to be ready to say goodbye, but that's what I'm doing now. I know you said that you want me back, but I'm afraid. Afraid of going through all of this again. The thing is, Hudson, I need a sign. I need a sign that getting back together is the right thing to do.

Until then, I'm going to say thank you and goodbye. Love, Alice."

"That was private," I say.

"I know," Hudson says.

He hands me the stack of thank-you cards and walks away. Slowly, the rest of the world comes into focus. Cars are honking. An ambulance is blaring. People are darting around me. The whole world that was nothing but background noise a minute ago, floods in. There's no room in it for me.

I ride the elevator back to the dorm completely numb. Doors open and close. People get in and out. They laugh and embrace and say goodbye. I see everything happening, but I don't understand any of it. They look like two-dimensional people. Characters. I wonder if they're real and how anyone would know for sure.

6

Juliet, Dylan, and I go out for drinks with a few other people from our floor. Apparently, Hudson texted Dylan and said that he'll be by later. I don't want to go, but I don't want to explain why I'm not going either.

The numbness finally starts to wear off after my second martini. Just at that precise moment, Hudson reappears. I see him standing in the doorway of the crowded bar full of celebrating college students. He's looking for someone. I turn to Juliet, trying to hide in my seat.

"Hudson's here!" Juliet and Dylan say almost simultaneously. Everyone cheers.

"Come join us, man," Dylan says. "You're about two drinks behind."

"Hey, everyone." He smiles. "I'm actually here to steal Alice away for a few minutes."

"No!" everyone replies jokingly. "Boo!"

"Alice." He comes closer to me, touching my back lightly. "Can I talk to you?"

I shake my head. Every time we've talked, things got worse and worse. Now, I'm not sure that our frail friendship will survive another one of our talks.

"Please, I have to talk to you," he whispers.

I sigh, take a sip of my martini, and eat an olive.

"You okay?" Juliet mouths to me silently. I shrug and follow Hudson out of the bar.

"Hudson, I want to apologize to you," I say, wrapping my scarf around my neck and zipping my coat. The air smells fresh and new, the cold's nipping at my nose. Every tree on the street is lit up in yellow lights. The city is screaming that Christmas is just around the corner.

"I do, too," he says. "Before we do any of that, I want to show you something. Will you come with me?"

Begrudgingly, I agree.

We walk back to our dorm, ride the elevator all the way to the top. I've never been this high before. He opens a small passageway with stairs leading even higher.

"Where are we going?" I finally ask.

"The roof."

"I didn't even know this place existed. Or that we could go here," I say.

"We can't. Not really, but I know one of the janitors and he let me up here before."

Still not into you

We walk out onto the roof.

"What do you do up here?" I ask.

"Think, mostly. It's a nice place for that. Quiet. Peaceful," he says.

Darkness falls with a vengeance in New York, quickly and without apologies. It doesn't dilly-dally. One minute it's daytime and the next it's nighttime and the world is lit up by lights.

"It looks like Christmas all the time here, doesn't it?" Hudson asks.

"What do you mean?"

"The lights. There are so many lights here. It's like it's Christmas all the time."

I've never thought of it that way before, but he's right. Every night, when the lights come on, the city seems to celebrate. Rejoice.

"Alice, I brought you up here because I want to show you something."

He takes a moment to collect his thoughts. I wait.

"I'm tired of simply telling you how I feel. I think I've used up all the words I have. So, I want to show you, instead."

He pauses again. Looks straight into my eyes and continues.

"Ever since I read that thank-you card, I've been going over all the ways that I've disappointed you. All the times that I've acted like a jerk and I think it all started that day, about a week after we broke up. When we were first trying to be friends.

We were supposed to see a movie together, remember?"

I nod. Of course, I remember.

"They were having a special showing of *Titanic* and I had promised to take you to see it. Then I didn't show up."

I had waited for half an hour. Then went inside and cried through the whole movie.

"It's fine," I say. "Ancient history."

"No, it's not fine. I was an inconsiderate dick and I'm sorry."

I nod. Hudson never really apologized for that. Not in a way that let me believe him.

"Thank you," I say. "I really appreciate it."

"So, I want to do something to make up for that," he says.

Hudson takes my hand, turns me around. There's a projector pointed at a big white screen and two lounge chairs in front of it. Large, warm blankets cover the chairs and a small table in the front with a bottle of wine, two glasses, and a plate of cheese and crackers.

"What is this?" I turn to Hudson.

"It's my apology. For everything," he says. "For ever hurting your feelings and for letting you go."

My chest tightens up. For a second, I feel like the wind has been knocked out of me.

"Alice, I don't want to just be your first boyfriend," he says. "I want to be your boyfriend again."

Still not into you

I sit down on the chair. He wraps the blanket around me, pours me a glass of wine. Hudson pulls his chair close to mine. I look up at him. I watch the way his breath moves in the cold air. He starts the movie. We watch in silence for a little while. When Rose gets out of the car in her fabulous hat and heads toward the ship, I turn to Hudson.

"Okay," I whisper.

He smiles at me, shaking his head. Like he doesn't believe me.

I lean over. He takes my hand, wrapping his fingers around mine. His fingers are hot to the touch; mine are as cold as ice. Hudson brings my fingers to his lips and lightly blows on them. His mouth spreads warmth throughout my entire body.

He moves even closer. We breathe the same air. I close my eyes and feel his lips on mine. A spark of electricity courses through me.

"I love you," he whispers through the kiss.

"I love you, too."

Dear Alice,

Thank you.

Thank you for opening up yourself to love again. You don't know what's going to happen in the future, but you have taken a leap of faith. You were afraid, but you didn't let that stop you from doing what you felt was right. I've always thought that to show courage was to run into a burning building to save a life. Well, by opening myself up to love again, I've run into a burning building and saved a life. My own.

Love,
Alice

7

When I arrive at JFK Airport for my second semester at Columbia University that spring, I breathe in the crisp January air and realize that this city has become something of an old friend. Familiar. Not so friendly. A little too grumpy. Almost always too loud. Despite all the shortcomings—or maybe because of them—New York is the kind of old friend you start to miss if you're not around her for a bit.

People come here to leave their mark, but I'm not so sure that it's the people who leave their mark on this city or if it is the other way around. It shaped me, defined me, forced me to confront my true self. Examine who I am and what I want to be.

This city came into my life and changed me. It morphed me into an adult. I complained and kicked and screamed, but the city didn't give up on me. It taught me to live on my own and do all the little tasks that come with growing: laundry, grocery shopping, getting your own medicine from the pharmacy when you're sick.

New York is full of ghosts—ghosts you feel when you wander the streets at twilight. You can feel them in the morning, too, when the city's just waking up. The ghosts are not just of the dead, for this city keeps souls, souls of those who come for a week and those who stay for years.

Walking out of the airport, I suddenly realize that there's a clear line between home and school. It should be obvious, of course. Calabasas is a place an hour north of Los Angeles where oranges dot the landscape in the winter and the sky is so wide and blue that it's easy to forget what day, month, and year it is. It's a place that the sun isn't fearful of. It's a place that rain rarely visits. School, on the other hand, is an entirely different world. Here, the streets explode in a cacophony of sounds I never knew existed. It's a place where bakeries open at 5 a.m. and bars and clubs don't close until 4 a.m. It's a place where people seem to live more fully at night than they do during the day. Unlike back home, where even a few drops of rain usually cancel all plans for the day, here the streets can be wet, full of slush, and covered in snow, but that doesn't stop anyone from going wherever they were going.

As I get into the cab, I'm excited at the prospect

Still not into you

of coming back to my new home here in the city. For one thing, my roommates are no longer strangers, but friends. Old friends. Like that old Dolly Parton song goes, "you can't make old friends." Unlike my first semester here, this time around, no introductions are needed. We're going to start off right where we had left off. Laughing. Talking. Reminiscing. I can't wait.

From what I heard, Dylan Waterhouse, my roommate who grew up in Connecticut and whose father owns a posh apartment overlooking Central Park, is back with Peyton, his high school girlfriend. Dylan and Peyton, who goes to Yale, had broken up and got back together numerous times last semester. According to Juliet, my roommate from Staten Island whose father owns a string of dry cleaners, they had gotten back together and broken up twice over Christmas break. I guess they're going through an on period. All this drama gives Juliet an insane amount of delight, despite the fact that she and Dylan had a thing for close to a month last semester and I was expecting her to be a little bitter over the whole thing.

The thing that's even better than old friends is an old love. My old love, to be precise. I haven't seen Hudson since we had gone skiing on New Year's.

"Alice!" Hudson yells as I get out of the cab in front of our building. He wraps his arms around me as I try to fish out a $10 bill to tip the cab driver.

He has recently shaved. His skin feels smooth and smells of coconut oil, his DIY aftershave. I wrap my arms around him and hug him as tightly as I can. Then…my heart jumps into my throat. I take a breath. My chest hurts and no air comes in. My heart starts to beat faster and faster. One more second and it'll pop out of my chest.

"What's wrong? You okay?" Hudson asks.

He pulls away from me.

"I'm sorry. I'm just…" I mumble. "I can't breathe."

"Oh my God, Alice. What's wrong?"

"Nothing." I shake my head. "I just need a minute."

I double over and put my head in between my knees. I've never had a panic attack, but that's what I heard Dr. Drew say to do in situations like these. Hudson patiently pats my back and waits.

I take one deep breath. Then another. Slowly, my heartbeat returns to normal. It hits me. It's love. I'm actually overwhelmed by love.

"Okay, I'm good." I stand up straight. I'm no longer sweating, but I'm suddenly keenly aware of how sweaty I am. My shirt is soaked and I'm getting colder with every second. Hudson stares at me with his brows furrowed and his face as serious as I've ever seen it. He's concerned.

"Sorry about that," I say. "I just got a little too excited about seeing you, I guess."

Still not into you

He takes me into his arms again.

"Are you okay?" he whispers.

"Yeah." I nod. "I think that was a mini-panic attack or something. No worries. It's over."

I look up at Hudson's face. At the end of last semester, his tan had started to wear off, but now, it's back again. It's almost certainly from surfing and skiing over Christmas break. I take a moment to admire how nice his body feels next to mine. Even through all the layers of clothes, his arms feel strong and powerful. His piercing eyes sparkle under the lights of the city and alternate between hazel and green, depending on the angle.

Hudson's light brown hair is longer than it was last semester, falling into his face. I move a few strands out of his face. My fingers brush over his lips, which are glittering and soft despite the cold weather and lack of Chapstick. He purses them and kisses my fingers lightly. Then he pulls me closer. Tilting my head upward, he kisses me. His tongue brushes across my upper lip and my knees grow weak. We start to move in unison, as if we're dancing to the same melody. My breaths match his breaths. His shoulders drop at the same time as mine rise. It's a game of give and take, with neither of us giving or taking too much.

A sudden gust of wind assaults us, bringing us back to reality for a moment. It's almost 10:30 p.m. and twenty-three degrees on Broadway in January.

"Let's go inside," Hudson whispers without pulling away from my lips.

"Okay," I mumble back. This is our special game—talking through our kisses. It's something we have done forever and it's one of the things that I love most about us.

8

We go upstairs. Juliet, Peyton, and Dylan are there, hanging out in the living room. Juliet and I share one room; Dylan and Hudson share another. We all share the living room, kitchen, and bathroom. After a ton of hugs and kisses, the guys serve us all drinks and we catch up or rather, I catch up. Everyone else has been here for a few hours already and, from the looks of it, the drinks were already flowing.

I haven't seen Juliet since December and I'm taken aback by how beautiful her hair is. Juliet is a voluptuous brunette with porcelain skin and to-die-for silky hair. I don't know how she makes her hair so shiny, but I'm jealous. She gave me all of her products to use last semester, but my hair never got that lustrous, no matter what I did.

Dressed in high heel boots, a tight turtleneck sweater, and a short black skirt, Juliet is the epitome of chic. I, on the other hand, look like the '90s threw up on me. I'm wearing leggings, a shabby t-shirt that's way too thin for this weather, and a plaid button down shirt.

Dylan hands me a beer. He's dressed in his usual uniform—a Nautica sweater, loafers, and slacks.

"Hey, Dylan, do you own any other clothes?" Juliet asks as if she's reading my mind.

"What do you mean?" He shrugs.

"No, he doesn't." Peyton laughs.

"What's wrong with what I'm wearing?" Dylan asks, looking down at his clothes.

"You look like you just stepped off a sailboat in Nantucket." Peyton smiles.

She's making fun of him, but it's obvious that she loves him and his clothes. He's an L. L. Bean cover model and she's the Connecticut queen on his arm.

Come to think of it, Juliet and Peyton could be sisters. They have almost identical chocolate hair, similar disapproving looks, and opinionated, know-it-all, coy smiles. Except that Juliet's a lot curvier than Peyton. That's really an understatement. Peyton's so thin, she's practically malnourished, and that's coming from someone who lives in LA.

Dylan and Juliet play beer pong while Peyton's nose is stuck in her phone. The fact that Juliet and Dylan are still on good terms is shocking to me. I mean, they slept together for over a month last semester after Peyton fell in love with her Resident

Advisor at Yale. Yet, here they all are—Dylan and Peyton are back together without bruised egos or hard feelings and Juliet and Dylan are friends again. Honestly, they're the epitome of some sort of post-relationship awakening—the image of modernity.

"Okay, kids," Juliet says, finishing her beer. "It's been fun catching up, but I've got to go. I have a date."

"You've only been here a day and you're already going out?" I ask.

"Hey, mama's gotta play." She shrugs.

"So, who's your date?" Hudson asks.

"His name's Brayden. He's a stockbroker," Juliet announces in her usual way. Name, then occupation or major. I'm Alice, English major. Dylan is Dylan, undecided. Hudson is Hudson, economics major.

As soon as Juliet leaves, Hudson nudges me to go unpack in my room. I smile and tell everyone that we're going to go unpack. They all nod and pretend they don't know what we're going to do.

"You think you're so mysterious," I say when we're both alone in my room.

"No, not really." He shrugs and pulls me close to him. "I just want to be alone with you."

Hudson presses his lips onto mine. My knees grow weak again. Shivers run up and down my body.

"No, no, no." I shake my head. "I do actually have a lot of unpacking to do."

I pull away from him and unwrap his arms from my body. When I lean over my suitcase, he's around me again. Holding me tight. Close. I feel my body temperature rising.

"Where do you think you're going?" he whispers in his most soothing voice. I smile. Turn around to face him. It's not that I don't want him. I do. More than anything.

"What do you want?" I ask. The huge smile on my face is so wide, it's hurting my face, but I can't make it vanish.

"You," he says and tosses me onto the bed. "You're as light as a feather!" Hudson adds, the words that every girl dreams of hearing.

He climbs on top of me, cradles my head. He moves my hair off my neck and kisses my ear lightly. His kisses send shivers down my body and make my feet feel numb.

I lift his head up to my lips and kiss him on the mouth. I bury my hands in his hair. His hands remain at my sides, but his lips move along with mine. I feel him push into me.

I hear footsteps outside the door.

"What's that?" I ask, pushing him away.

"Nothing," he mumbles and starts to kiss my neck again. He gives me light little kisses along my collarbone, driving me wild, but something at the door is worrying me.

Still not into you

"What if Juliet comes back?" I ask.

"She won't," he says without stopping. "She's on her date."

"So, who's that? Outside?" I ask.

"Shhh." He puts his finger across my lips. "That's just Dylan and Peyton. They won't come in."

"How do you know?" I ask. I don't know what's worrying me, but something is making me stall. I'm trying to buy time. Why?

"They won't come in because I never intrude on them. They owe me."

I know he's right. I take a deep breath. Just relax. I've done this a million times. We've done this a million times. This is Hudson. You love him and he loves you.

As Hudson's mouth makes its way from my collarbone further down to my breasts and then around my ribs and down to my belly button, I start to relax. All thoughts of intruders suddenly vanish and I'm calm.

Wordlessly, Hudson pulls off my shirt and undoes my bra. He stands above me as he pulls off his own shirt. He isn't flexing, but the muscles in his stomach still make a perfect six-pack.

"You're so hot," I say, running my fingers over each pack.

"You're not so bad yourself," he says, snuggling out of his jeans. He kisses me lightly along my hipbones and tugs at the top of my leggings. I'm getting warm in between my legs. I lift up my butt to help him pull them off me. With one quick swoosh, I'm suddenly completely naked. No leggings, panties, or socks.

Hudson presses his body close to mine.

"You feel nice," he mumbles as we start to move in unison. I thread my fingers into his hair. His thick hair is so silky that my fingers can't seem to find traction.

He kisses me behind the ear as he finds his way into me. We fumble around at first, trying to find the right pace but quickly start to move together. Energy builds up within me. I let out a moan.

"I love you," he moans into my ear.

"I love you, too," I whisper as he sends me over the edge. I curl my toes as warmth pulsates throughout my body. I close my eyes and disappear into another world. Hudson moves faster and faster until he collapses on top of me.

My mind goes blank as my body goes limp. I can't feel the lower half of my body.

"Thank you," he says, sighing and rolling over next to me.

"No, thank you," I mumble.

9

We lie quietly next to each other for some time before either of us speaks again. It's still hard to believe that I'm lying here, next to *him*.

Hudson Hilton.

The guy who was my best friend for many years until one afternoon when he kissed me and we became more than friends. In high school, I thought he was the love of my life. When his family moved up to the Bay Area in the beginning of our senior year, my heart broke into a thousand pieces. He promised me that we would make it. We would go away to college together and we would be together forever. After we finally made it through that year apart, when we got into the same school and almost had everything we had ever dreamed of, we broke up. No, that's not true. I say that to make myself feel better, but it was really he who broke up with me.

The world turned to black and there was nothing I could do to bring life into it. Then things got worse. I came to college thinking I would start over, but found out that he was going to be my roommate.

"Isn't this crazy?" I ask. Neither of us bothers to put on any clothes, but I pull the comforter up. It's getting cold and the radiator is all the way across the room.

"What?" he asks. "Us?"

I nod.

"Yeah, it is," Hudson says with a smile. He rolls over to his side and props his head up with his hand.

"I don't have any regrets, do you?"

I shake my head. A part of me wishes that he had regretted ever breaking up with me. Another part thinks that maybe that whole thing made us stronger. We both learned something. We both dated people, experienced what it would be like to be out there. Seeing other people.

"I don't mean to bring up something bad," he says, choosing his words carefully. "But I sort of wish that we never broke up last summer. It was stupid."

I shrug and flash him a smile. It makes me so happy to hear that, I feel myself beaming.

"Why are you grinning like that?" he asks.

"Why do you think?" I ask.

"Because you were right?" he asks.

"I guess. Though those are your words, not mine."

Still not into you

He rolls his eyes and kisses me on the nose. I snuggle up in his armpit and close my eyes. I love the way things are now. Different, new, exciting. In ways that I'd never imagined possible.

Hudson and I spend the weekend before classes start hanging out. We get our textbooks, go out for brunch, walk around Riverside Park, and go shopping in Chinatown. Mostly, we laugh. We laugh like we haven't laughed in a long time. Like old friends who are just catching up. Everything and every story is exciting. We reminisce about high school. About sneaking out of gym class to go out to lunch. About making out in the church's parking lot late at night. About watching *Jaws* together in his parents' bed when no one was home. By the time Sunday night rolls around, I realize that I'm no longer holding my breath. I'm breathing easily. I didn't know it at the time, but our time together over Christmas break felt like a dream. I knew it was happening, but a big part of me almost didn't believe it. Now that we are back in school and together and happy, I'm no longer waiting for the other shoe to drop. It's like something heavy has been removed from my chest—something I didn't even know was there.

I'M TAKING sixteen credits this semester. Writing 101, a required composition class for freshmen,

Victorian literature, an advanced elective that I was lucky to get into, Introduction to Anthropology, another requirement—I think it fills the civilization requirement, but I'm not sure—and Public Speaking. Public Speaking is also required, and this is the class that I'm looking forward to the least or rather, not at all.

Public speaking gives me heart palpitations. It makes me shiver (not in a good way!) and makes me want to throw up. I'm not a public speaker. I'm terrified of giving speeches. I'm so bad at it that sometimes when I raise my hand in class, if the professor doesn't call on me immediately, I start to freak out and drop my hand and don't participate at all.

"I'm sorry, Alice, but you can't drop this class," my counselor informs me when I barge into her office without an appointment and try to weasel out of it. "Unfortunately, Public Speaking is one of the only classes that fulfills the diversity requirement and fits your schedule. If you didn't want this class, you should've thought about this last semester."

"The thing is that last semester, I thought I'd be brave. I thought that it would be good for me to take it and get over this fear, once and for all. But now that I actually have to go to class, I just don't think I can do it. I'm going to have a heart attack."

"You're going to be just fine, Alice." She smiles at me and ushers me outside. "I'm sorry, but I can't talk about this anymore. I have a lot of people

Still not into you

waiting. If you would like to schedule an appointment..."

"No, thank you for your time." I shake my head. "I'll be fine."

I lie. I'm not going to be fine. I'm going to fail.

I MEET Hudson for a late lunch after class. It's worse than I even imagined.

"I thought the professor would lecture for a bit and we would speak in public later. Like later in the semester. But no. I have to make a speech next week!" I say.

I'm jumbling my words together. I can barely breathe at the very thought.

"You're going to be fine," he says, patting my shoulders.

Why do people keep saying this? How do they know this? It's not a given.

"I have to make five speeches!" I say. "What am I going to do, Hudson? I'm going to die."

Hudson smiles. "You're not going to die."

He's not mocking me, but I'm not sure that he's getting the severity of this problem either.

"I'll help you prepare," he says. "You'll be fine."

"You will?" I ask. I like the sound of that.

Public speaking is not a big deal for Hudson. He was our class president for three years before he moved up north. Speaking in front of people doesn't faze him. He doesn't fear what others think of him. I wish I could be like that. Confident. Self-assured. I'm not and the more I want to be like that, the more embarrassed I get over how I really am.

"My first speech is next week," I say. "I have to give a toast."

"To whom?" he asks.

"Whomever I want. But I can't. No, I have to figure out a way to drop this class."

"No, you don't." He smiles at me. A confident, self-assured smile. "I'll help you. We'll get through this together."

Something about the way he says that puts me at ease. He's telling the truth and I believe him. I'm not doing this alone. I'll be doing this with him. We'll be doing it together. It's always easier to do things together, right? I suddenly feel like this is actually possible.

10

"So, I'm starting the internship tomorrow," Hudson says after our pizza is ready.

We only ordered two slices, but the slices are so large at this place they take up half the table. Thin crust with a thin layer of fresh mozzarella and veggies. Delicious.

"Young's and Associates, right?" I ask, taking a big bite of my slice. He nods.

"Three days per week," he adds. "Full days."

"That's intense," I say. "But exciting, right?"

He shrugs. He's anxious about this. I've never really seen him this way.

"What if I'm no good?" he asks. I shake my head.

"Impossible."

He smiles.

Young's and Associates is an investment bank on Wall Street. The internship is very prestigious and ridiculously competitive. He found out that he got in over Christmas break. In addition to the internship, he's also taking a full load of classes. Hard classes. Calculus II and Macroeconomics and a couple of requirements.

"How are you going to manage?" I ask.

"Somehow, I guess. It's such a great opportunity. I just don't want to mess it up."

"So, when are you taking classes then, if the internship is all day long?"

"I had to rearrange my schedule today. I'm not taking any classes on the days I'm working. So, they're all crammed into the evenings and two are three hours long on Thursdays and Fridays."

"Wow, that sucks!" I sympathize. "Is it all semester?"

He nods.

"Until May. Then if it all goes well and I do really well, I'll be in the running for their full-time summer internship."

"That's a lot of free labor they're getting out of college students," I say.

"I guess." He shrugs. "I know I'm going to learn a lot. Plus, it will set me up well for getting a good job after graduation."

I'm impressed by his drive, but I can't lie, the schedule puts me off.

"What's wrong?" he asks.

"Nothing." I shrug. I can tell that he doesn't believe me. "Well, it's not that I'm not happy for you. I am. I just don't want you to get overwhelmed. I mean, this is college. I want you to have time for fun and your friends."

"And you." He finishes my sentence.

"That's not what I said," I say, even though that's what I meant.

"Don't worry." He gives me a kiss on my cheek. "I'll make time for us. I'm not going to work too hard."

"Okay." I nod.

The following night, I don't see Hudson until 7 p.m. He's at his internship all day and then I get a text that he's going to happy hour with his associates after work. I won't admit it out loud, but I'm annoyed. It's only the first day and it's already irritating me. I hate that I want him to spend time with me. Make time for me. I don't want to be that girl; I want to be supportive and steadfast, but I'm not. The best I can do is keep my mouth shut.

"Guess what?" Hudson asks me that night after he comes home. "I didn't have to use my fake ID downtown."

"Really?"

"Apparently, those bartenders don't card anyone in a suit. At least, according to Kathryn."

"Who's Kathryn?"

"Oh, she's just one of the people I work with. She's quite impressive actually. She graduated from NYU's Stern School of Business last year. She worked at Young's for three summers while she was in college before they hired her. She's really driven."

I shrug and nod. Suddenly, I get a strange feeling about the whole thing. Like the existence of Kathryn will play a significant role in the events that are about to take place.

THE NEXT AFTERNOON, I walk into the one class that I'm really excited about taking this semester: Victorian Literature. I can't believe that I have actually been going around calling myself an English major and I have never read *Pride and Prejudice* or anything by Charles Dickens. That's one of the reasons I'm so excited about the class. I'm sure that it will fix all of my literary shortcomings.

"Hey!" Tea says, sitting down in the seat next to mine with a big, wide smile across her face.

I'm just as happy to see her.

"I was hoping you'd be in this class," I say.

Tea and I met last semester. After a few awkward weeks when she and Hudson were sort of dating and Hudson was refusing to define their relationship or be exclusive, Tea and I developed quite a friendship.

"You look really good," I say, looking her up and down. Tea has always had a gorgeous face, the kind that would have Renaissance painters swooning. Now, she's even more radiant.

Still not into you

"Thanks for noticing." She blushes. "I lost twenty-three pounds. I'm a size twelve now."

"Wow, that's amazing." I smile. "I'm so proud of you."

"I haven't been a size twelve since ninth grade."

I nod. Tea is one of those beautiful big women who you'd never know was unhappy with her weight. While I have a tendency to slouch, she always stands up straight.

"I do feel like I lost it all in my boobs though." She laughs, grabbing her 36 DDs.

"What inspired you to do all this?" I ask.

"I got home from school in December, stepped on the scale, and discovered that I was 198 pounds. That's almost 200! I've never been so heavy in my whole life. So, I knew that I had to do something about it. Quick."

I look at her body a little closer. Her waistline is more defined and her breasts are perky and sit higher on her body than they used to. Her eyes don't look so tired anymore either. Even her skin has a kind of glow to it. Though the last two things could really be because it's the first week of the new semester, not finals week. I'm sure that my eyes aren't that tired right now either.

"Oh. I have more news," she whispers as the professor introduces herself and passes out the syllabus.

"I'm dating someone now!" she says with a little shriek at the end.

"Who?"

"This guy. His name is Tanner. He's a grad student in architecture."

I'm so happy for her. She's a really good girl and she deserves to find someone who can appreciate her for her.

"What about you? You seeing anyone special?" she asks.

My heart jumps into my throat. I should've expected this question, but for some reason I didn't.

I don't know why, but I didn't expect to talk about Hudson. This is the only thing that's weird in our relationship. I like Tea a lot and I know that we can even be closer than we are now. Except that there's Hudson. Guys always get in the way.

I mouth "later" and pretend that I'm listening to what the professor has to say. I don't want to answer her question. I don't know how she'll react, but I know that it will be a defining moment. If she's upset, we probably won't be friends. No matter how hard I try. If she doesn't care, then we'll be okay.

The professor is giving an introduction about Charles Dickens. The importance of *Oliver Twist* for his society and how that book redefined the way the society thought about poverty and child labor and workhouses. It's fascinating, don't get me wrong, but I can't quiet my mind. It keeps going back to Tea's question. All I can think about is how I'm going to tell Tea about Hudson, and whether I even should. I mean, I could lie. I could pretend that everything's

Still not into you

fine. That we're just friends. I'm sure that I can even get Hudson to go along with it. He wouldn't really care either way, but then what would we have? Would we really be friends if I'm hiding this big part of my life from her?

By the end of class, I come to a decision. Yes, I'm going to tell her. It's better to just tell the truth. I don't know if she would find out either way, but at least we would be friends for the right reasons then. If we won't be friends, that's fine, too. I mean, it was Tea who dumped him for not wanting to commit to being her boyfriend and she does have a new boyfriend now. Maybe it will all work out or maybe not. I'm starting to waver…

Class ends and my decision isn't as steadfast as it was a few minutes ago. Shit. I take a deep breath and tell her the truth.

"Hudson? You're seeing Hudson?"

I nod and shrug my shoulders. I look away from her. I don't want to see her reaction, in case it's bad.

"Oh, wow, that's cool," she says. I hear a little awkwardness in her voice, but that's to be expected, I guess.

"I hope that's okay," I say. I don't mean for it to come out as if I'm asking her permission. That's not what I mean.

"Oh, yes of course. I mean, we're not together. In comparison to you two, we barely dated at all. He wouldn't even call whatever we had dating. So, it's nothing."

I finally look at her face, straight on. She's telling the truth. I can see by the way her face is hiding nothing. Better yet, she seems to be genuinely happy for me. The tension at the back of my neck dissipates immediately. I take a big sigh of relief.

"I'm glad you're okay with this," I say.

"Yes, definitely." She grins.

"I just wasn't sure how you would react and I didn't want us to lose this…our friendship. It means a lot to me."

Tea smiles from ear to ear.

"No, of course not. No matter what, we're not going to let a guy come in between us," she says.

"No, of course not." I shake my head.

"Well, let's hang out sometime," she says. "Okay?"

"Okay." I nod. "I'd love that."

Lots of people make plans to see each other soon without really meaning it. It's just the nice thing to do. I've done it myself a million times. This feels different. I know that we both mean it.

11

The second week of school goes by just as quickly as the first. A little too quickly, actually. I have to make my first speech that Friday. The toast. I don't want the day to come. I've been thinking about it for days but once the Monday before rolls around, I feel myself getting terrified. On Monday, I'm still able to manage the fear. I try to deal with it by convincing myself that it'll be okay. On Monday, I believe it. Unfortunately, by Wednesday, all of my arguments stop working. I just feel like I'm going to have a heart attack every time I think about it, which is practically all day long.

On Wednesday, I decide that I need some practice. Maybe saying the words out loud will make me feel a little better. I stand up in front of the mirror. I look down at the notes that I wrote down but can't read a thing. When I open my mouth, my voice shakes. Supposedly, I memorized the words earlier or I thought I did. Now that I have to speak out loud, just to myself, nothing comes to mind. I can't even remember how I planned on starting.

The worst thing about all of this is that Hudson is nowhere to be found. He had promised me that we would practice together. He promised me this originally at lunch and cancelled on me all weekend. We made plans on Saturday and then Sunday and then Monday night. By the time it was Tuesday, I didn't bother making plans anymore. He came home late that night, around 9 p.m., and said that he had a ton of Macroeconomics to catch up on.

Come to think of it, I haven't even seen him since Wednesday morning when we waited for our Pop-Tarts to toast together. Agh, what makes me so mad is that he had promised that he would practice with me, help me. Now it's 9:30 p.m. on Thursday and he's still not back. He has yet to help me once. I'm angry and disappointed. Mostly, I'm scared. The speech is tomorrow and I have nothing.

"Dylan, I think I'm going to have a heart attack," I say, coming out of my room into the living room. Dylan's playing something on the Xbox. Without looking up, he asks what's wrong and I give him the highlights.

"You'll do fine," he says, finally putting the controller down. I watch him as he walks to the refrigerator and gets a soda.

Why does everyone say that when they don't

Still not into you

even know what's going on? There's NO way I'm going to do fine. People who freeze and can't say a word out loud don't do fine in public speaking classes.

I shake my head. "No way," I say.

"Well, you were going to do it with Hudson, right? So why not me?" he asks.

"Because…there's like a million reasons why not," I say.

"Name one," he challenges me.

"I don't know." I shrug. "But this is worse than being naked. In fact, I think I'd rather be naked with someone than do this."

"Oh, really?" His eyes light up in a mischievous way. "Well, then, we can arrange that."

"Agh, you're a pig." I roll my eyes. "You know what I mean."

"Okay, okay, I get it."

"The thing is that I'm terrified. I can't do it." I shrug.

"But you were going to do it with Hudson?" he asks.

"I said I would, but I'm not sure I actually would have gone through with it. I think I was just going to try."

"Well, why don't you try for me?" Dylan asks. "I'll help you. I'm great at speeches."

"That doesn't surprise me," I say.

"I know, right?" He laughs. "My dad says that

I'm the king of bullshitting. That's why he wants me to go to law school."

"Wow, that's a great reflection on this country's legal system," I say.

"Eh, I guess," he says, unfazed. "I'm actually thinking of doing it. Seriously."

"Wow, this is like the most honest, non-bullshitty conversation I think we've ever had," I say.

"First time for everything," he says sarcastically.

"So, what's keeping you back?" I ask. "From actually pursuing the path to law school?"

"Well, for one, there's no real path. I mean, I can major in whatever and I won't be taking the LSAT until my junior year," he says. "What's really keeping me from it is that I know it'll make my dad happy and that's the last thing I want."

I smile. The moment has passed. Sincerity is out of the window. Now the real Dylan's back.

"Okay, enough stalling," he says. "I want to hear this toast."

Damn it. I open my crumpled piece of paper. Clear my throat. As soon as my eyes drop down to the first line, at the top, my heart starts to pound loudly. Suddenly, it's the only thing that I can hear in my head. I try to ignore it. I open my mouth, but nothing comes out. My throat is dry, like a desert. I feel like I haven't drunk a drop of liquid in days.

"Okay, okay," Dylan says, cutting off my suffering. He takes the paper out of my hand.

Still not into you

"Alice, look at me. Why are you so scared?" he asks. He's staring straight into my eyes.

"I have no idea," I whisper.

"Do you think I'm going to laugh at you? Mock you? Heckle you?" Dylan asks.

No, of course not. I shake my head. He waits for me to reply.

"I have no idea," I mumble.

"Well, I'm not going to do any of those things. I'm here just to sit and listen and clap."

Something about someone even listening scares the crap out of me.

"I hope not too attentively," I say with a shrug.

"Why do you think that you're so unimportant?" Dylan asks.

There's clarity in his voice, the kind that only appears when you hit upon the truth. I guess a big part of me does think that I'm unimportant. I mean, I don't even want anyone to hear what I have to say. That's pretty pathetic.

"Okay, how about this?" Dylan changes tactics. "There are freshmen in this class, right?"

I nod.

"Well, then, they probably don't even care what you have to say. They're going to be checking their phones. Barely look up at you, let alone actually listen to you."

"The thought of that does make me feel a lot better," I say with a little sigh of relief. Quickly old fears creep in and whatever mild feeling of apathy I managed to scrounge up disappears.

"Okay, I don't feel better anymore. Just as scared as before," I tell him.

"This is crazy," Dylan says with a smile. He shakes his head. I can see that he's perplexed by this whole thing. "I didn't know anyone could be in such bad shape," he says, shaking his head. "Okay, let's forget about this for a little bit."

Dylan puts my pitiful, crumpled, and used up speech on the kitchen counter.

"What are you doing?" I ask. "Are you giving up on me? No, you can't!"

Panic sets in. If he gives up on me, then I have no one.

"No, I'm not giving up on you." Dylan shakes his head. "We just need a break."

He opens the fridge and hands me a beer.

"No, I can't drink now," I say, shaking my head. "I'm too freaked out by all this."

"You have to. You're psyching yourself out. It'll make you feel better."

"I have this speech tomorrow. I need to figure out a way to get through it," I say.

"And you will, but for now, you need to relax and not freak out so much. Clear your head."

Despite my better judgment, I end up having two beers. We watch *Watch What Happens Live* and play a drinking game with Andy Cohen. I'm a real lightweight when it comes to drinking and even one

Still not into you

drink gets me tipsy. So, after two, I'm nice and buzzed. My muscles loosen, my shoulders let up, and most importantly, my mind finally quiets down. I'm finally able to think in complete sentences—my thoughts are no longer running like crazy.

During a commercial break, Dylan hands me my speech.

"What are you doing?" I ask, laughing. He doesn't say a word, just nudges it toward me.

At first, I pick up the paper as a joke. I laugh a little. I look down at my hands. I expect them to shake just like they did before, but they're steady. I read the words. Much to my surprise, they all make sense. No thoughts of failure and disappointment trickle in. Instead, I feel a distinct sense of apathy. I don't really care what Dylan thinks of what I have to say. It's pretty good and that's enough for me. Whatever he thinks can't hurt me.

I start off by reading the first line. When it comes out right, I go on to the next and the next. By the end of the first paragraph, I'm talking in a normal speaking voice. I'm even pausing for effect and looking up at Dylan to see if he's paying attention. By the time I'm close to the end, whatever jitters I had are all gone. Not because I'm done speaking, but because I just don't particularly care what Dylan thinks.

"Awesome!" Dylan says, clapping his hands after I finish. "That was amazing. You were amazing!"

"Wow." I shake my head. For a moment, I have

an out of body experience. I don't feel like it was actually me who spoke up there.

"See, you can do this!" Dylan says, giving me a warm hug. "You just need to get out of your own way. Not think about the process so much. Let yourself go."

12

The following afternoon, I arrive to Public Speaking class early. I've had two beers the hour before. It's undeniable—I feel loose and confident and a little apathetic (that's a good thing, according to Dylan). I also feel guilty. A big part of me, the part I try to suppress with all of my might, thinks this is cheating. I need to go into this cold or not at all, but I know what's going to happen if I go in cold. If I couldn't do it in front of Dylan, there's no way I'm going to be able to do it in front of a room of strangers and Professor Milner.

I need to get this over with, I say to myself. The sooner the better. So, when Professor Milner asks for volunteers, I raise my hand. Without two beers in me, I would never volunteer for this. Instead, I would pray that I wouldn't be called on next and if time runs out in class, I would take a big sigh of relief and then fret and worry about this for another week. Now, I'm different. I'm braver. Bolder. Not so afraid.

I go up to the podium. A class of thirty or so bored kids stare back at me. Professor Milner gives me a nod of encouragement. A girl in the front row types frantically on her phone. *I can do this*, I say to myself.

"Okay, everyone," I start. My voice is confident, self-assured. Just how it was last night. "Can I have your attention please?" I say. I'm giving a toast, and I pretend that I'm holding a glass in my left hand.

"I'd like to take this opportunity and congratulate Dylan and Peyton on their upcoming wedding. I've known Dylan for many years, ever since he was my roommate freshman year in college. Over the years, we grew up, changed, but one thing remained the same, steadfast: his love for Peyton. Anyone who knows them knows that they've had their share of breakups, but instead of letting that tear them apart, each breakup somehow made them stronger. I've had the privilege of knowing this couple for many years now and I know that they have loved each other for many, many years. Ever since high school. How many of us can say that we met the love of our life in high school? Not many, that's for sure. So, let's put our glasses up in honor of this blessed union. I love you both."

When I'm done, everyone in the class claps. I'm stunned. I still can't believe that I actually did that—

spoke out loud for a significant amount of time in front of a group of people. Did this really happen or am I going to wake up any minute now and realize that I still have to do the speech in a few hours?

As I make my way back to my desk, I feel my heart filling with pride. Who was that girl speaking so confidently in front of a room of strangers? It's not every day that you surprise yourself.

The girl who was texting during my speech gets up to give hers. My mind continues to spin, but in a good way. I'm in awe. In addition to my shock that I actually got through the toast in one piece, I'm also surprised about the content of the speech.

This was not the toast that I wrote the week before and it wasn't the toast that I practiced with Dylan last night. No, that toast was for Hudson on his birthday. Today at lunch, completely on a whim, I took five minutes and wrote a toast to Dylan. I wanted to thank him for helping me with the speech. I wouldn't have survived today were it not for him. I didn't have a good reason to thank him for anything, so I switched it up and wrote a wedding toast.

"Professor Milner actually said that I did a good job," I brag to Dylan that evening.

Hudson's warming up some soup in the microwave.

"Oh, was that today?" Hudson asks. He hadn't asked me about it before.

I hate the absentminded look on his face. I want to throw my plate at his head, but I restrain myself. This is my time to celebrate. This is a good thing. I'm in a good place. I'm on cloud nine. Nothing he does or doesn't do will change that.

"I'm sorry, I completely forgot," Hudson says.

I ignore him.

"Dylan, I was amazing. I had no inhibitions. Okay, very little. I said everything I wanted to say and all the words came out right. I even paused for dramatic effect!"

"That's great." Dylan grins ear to ear. "I knew you could do it."

"I knew you could do it, too," Hudson butts in.

"You should've heard her toast, Hudson," Dylan says. "It was to you on your birthday. She had really nice things to say."

"No, actually, it wasn't," I say.

"What? But that's what we had practiced."

"I know, but when I was going over it again at lunch, it just felt…off. So, I rewrote it. I congratulated you and Peyton on your upcoming wedding."

"What?!" Dylan gasps. Hudson also seems to be taken aback. "That's a scary thought," Dylan jokes.

Still not into you

"I know, I'm sorry. I just wanted to thank you. A wedding toast sounded right."

"Just as long as it's pretend," Dylan says, laughing all the way back to his room.

I'm about to walk back toward my room as well, but Hudson catches up with me.

"Hey, listen, I'm so, so sorry about this whole thing. I said I'd help and I didn't."

I shrug. I don't want to say that it was no big deal because it was. I also don't want to get into all this right now.

"I was just swamped with work and classes, but I know it's no excuse," Hudson says.

"I honestly don't know what I would've done were it not for Dylan. You really let me down," I say. "And Dylan saved me."

There's so much more to say. It's only the second week and Hudson's schedule is already impossible. I hate his new internship. I want him to quit. We don't have any time for each other and we're in college. If we don't have time for each other now, when will we?

I don't say any of those things. I don't want to cloud my celebration with a fight or even a disagreement.

13

The night after my first speech, Hudson promises to make more time for me. Unfortunately, he doesn't keep it. He continues to come back home later and later over the next few weeks. Sometimes even after midnight.

Eventually, I stop waiting up for him. I rarely see him in the mornings, too. He's usually gone before I get up.

"Honestly, I don't know how he survives on so little sleep," I finally vent to Juliet one night. "I don't know what's going on. He can't be working all this time, right?"

It's Monday night and we're watching *The Daily Show* and Hudson's still not back.

"I have a few friends who dated stockbrokers," she says, "and they do work crazy hours."

"What about that guy you had a date with? Did he?" I ask.

"I don't know." She shrugs. "I just saw him once."

I shake my head. Something doesn't feel right.

"So, you think it's fine?" I ask.

"Well, they work crazy hours, but not this crazy."

"He says that he has to go out every night because that's what everyone does," I say. Somehow, those words make a lot more sense when they come from him. It sounds completely unconvincing when I say it.

"Hey! I have an idea," Juliet says. I spot a dangerous twinkle in her eyes.

"What?" I ask cautiously.

"Why don't we follow him?"

"No," I say, shaking my head. "I'm not one of those jealous girlfriends."

"I know you don't want to see yourself like that, but difficult times call for dangerous measures," Juliet says. "Or however that saying goes."

I'm not convinced. I can't go along with this. Don't get me wrong, I want to know the truth, but I also don't. I know my heart will break if he's lying… and then what?

I shake my head no, decisively. I can't do this.

"You're entitled to know the truth, Alice. I mean, what if he's screwing around on you? Don't you want to know that?"

No, not really, I want to say. I'd rather not know it, but that sounds old-fashioned and hopeless and

Still not into you

pathetic. Most of all, not true. I do want to know. I just don't want to want to know.

"If it's nothing, then you won't be worrying about this so much. It's a win-win."

"It sounds like a lose-lose, actually," I say. "But okay."

THE FOLLOWING EVENING, we take a cab to The Martini. It's a bar that Hudson mentioned to me a couple of times, the place that they all go to after work for happy hour, the place where they don't card people in suits.

It's raining and I'm reluctant to put on a costume, but Juliet insists. So, I arrive at The Martini in professional-height heels, a white blouse, a black mini-skirt, and my jacket. It's the closest thing I have to an office wardrobe, and even this one I had to compile from Juliet's closet.

Juliet still straightens and then curls her hair and puts on fake lashes but I take a more relaxed approach. Eye shadow, eyeliner, mascara, lipstick. That's enough. If this night goes badly, I don't need to look like a clown when it all starts streaming down my face.

We walk into the bar around 6:30 p.m. It's still relatively empty and we find a dark, quiet table all the way in the back. This is a stakeout, so he's not supposed to see us immediately, if at all. Juliet quickly orders us two dirty martinis on the rocks with extra olives. On the way over, I promised myself that I would stay sober during this, but one drink doesn't mean I'll be drunk. When it arrives, I cave. I need something to calm my nerves and it fits the bill.

We wait and sit for a while before we see them. I'm not sure how long exactly, except that I finish my martini and Juliet finishes two. Then I see him.

Hudson, dressed in a suit, holds the door open for a woman. She's wearing a bright red peacoat and high-heel boots. She tosses her hair from side to side as if she's in a Pantene commercial.

"Who's that?" Julie asks.

"I don't know." I shrug. "Maybe this girl Kathryn."

"Who's Kathryn?"

"Just someone he works with."

"Well, I'm not sure that girl has ever been a 'just someone' ever," Juliet says.

I know exactly what she means. That girl is drop-dead gorgeous. She has light brown hair and expensive-looking highlights. She sits across from Hudson, facing us, and we get a clear view of her. She's beautiful. A small delicate mouth, high cheekbones, a perfectly contoured face.

"She reminds me of someone," Juliet says.

I shrug. I'm more interested in the way that she's leaning toward Hudson and laughing at everything he says.

Still not into you

"Kind of like a cross between Emily Blunt and Kate Middleton," Juliet says. "Oh my God! Do you see where she just put her hand? It's on his knee."

I nod, speechless. I really wish that I didn't bring Juliet along for this.

The woman doesn't keep her hand on his knee for long. It was just a pat, a tap, but it's enough to send me into a tailspin.

I'm lost. I don't know what I'm doing here. I can't move. I can't believe what I'm seeing. I want to get up and leave, but I don't.

In a moment, the place gets so crowded, I can barely see over all the people who are congregating around the bar.

"Where are you going?" Juliet asks as I grab my purse and phone.

"Home."

"No, you can't go home! We didn't see anything yet."

"Juliet, I can't do this anymore. He's going to do what he's going to do. I don't have to torture myself and watch."

Her eyes search my face for answers, but I don't have a better answer than that. It's not that I don't want to know. I just can't be in this place any longer. The walls feel like they're closing in on me. I fear that if I stay, I'm going to scream.

I make my way around the perimeter of the place. I'm not trying to avoid Hudson anymore—in fact, I don't care if he sees me, but the bar is so crowded, I couldn't even make my way over there if I tried.

"Alice," Juliet whispers somewhere behind me. "Alice!"

When I turn around, I see that Juliet is staring at something to her right. My eyes follow her gaze. Then I see them.

Hudson and the woman are laughing and they're so close to each other, their faces are almost touching. A moment later, she leans over and kisses him on the lips.

Everything suddenly feels like it's happening in third person. Not to me, but to someone who looks a lot like me on the screen. I'm suddenly outside without my coat. The chill of January hits me like a pile of bricks. I look around. I have to find a cab. I have to text Uber. My mind wanders in circles. I can't make a decision. All I'm decided about is that I can't go back in for my coat.

"Alice! Alice, wait up!" Juliet runs out after me. She hands me my coat.

"He pulled away from her. He stopped her," she says.

"What?" I ask, wrapping the scarf around my neck. I don't understand a word of what she's saying.

"She kissed him and he stopped her. He pulled right away. You just didn't see it," she says.

I pull my coat shut—the zipper is too complicated to operate at this moment.

Still not into you

"Is that supposed to make me feel better?" I ask.

Juliet shrugs. "Well, yes, actually," she says.

I guess. I guess that's something. Except that it doesn't really feel like a victory. I feel like I lost a long time ago. It feels like it's all a little too late.

Juliet and I take a cab home in silence. She tries to talk to me, but I cut her off. I can't. Talking just makes my thoughts cloudier and incomprehensible. Finally, we walk into our room. I climb into bed and hide under the covers. I just want the whole world to disappear. I'm still awake when I hear Hudson come back. I look at the time. It's about half an hour later. I want to talk to him, but I don't have the energy. When he peeks into my room, I pretend to be asleep.

14

The following day, I have another speech in Public Speaking class. I was planning on getting up early and practicing it before class, but I end up sleeping until lunch. I want to stay in bed all day, but I can't skip it; it's a huge portion of my grade. When my hands start to shake looking down at the paper with my script, I go to the kitchen and force myself to down two beers. They taste disgusting first thing in the morning. This worked last time. It has to work this time.

Walking over to class, I hope that I don't run into Hudson. He has class in this area and I just can't see him now. Not before I get this speech over with. When Professor Milner asks for volunteers, I raise my hand.

Walking to the front of the class, I feel like I'm going to throw up. Not because of my nerves, but the alcohol. I take a deep breath. You can do this, I say to myself. Thirty sets of bored eyes look up at the podium. They don't care what you have to say. Don't think. Just start talking. I unfold my speech. This speech is about gratefulness. We're supposed to thank someone for helping us do something important.

"Thank you for having me," I start. "I want to take a moment to thank my mother and father for…"

I stare at the paper. The words are there in black and white. All I have to do is say them out loud, but for some reason, I can't. They don't make any sense. I have an overwhelming urge to thank someone else.

"No, actually, I don't want to thank my mother and father. I'd like to take this time to thank my boyfriend, Hudson. Thank you, Hudson, for never being there for me. Thank you for wasting two years of my life in high school and then breaking up with me a couple of weeks before college. Thank you for 'accidentally' becoming my roommate and confusing me with all of your crap last semester and tricking me into thinking that you've changed. Most of all, thank you for this semester. Thank you for promising to help me with my speeches and leaving me high and dry. Thank you for pretending that you have a lot of important work to do when in reality you're just hanging out with that girl that looks a lot like Kate Middleton, from your office. Of course, thank you for mentioning how hot she actually is before I show up at the bar to spy on you.

Still not into you

That was really the cherry on top. That made me feel a lot better watching you two make out. Most of all, thank you for doing all of that now before I wasted even more of my life on you. You fucking asshole!"

Shit. What did I just say?

I look up at the class. Thirty pairs of hands start to clap and cheer. Oh my God! I nod, hang my head, and make my way back to my chair.

At least I didn't freeze. No, the words just came out. I couldn't make them stop. I definitely shouldn't have cursed.

After class ends, I try to make my way outside, past the professor, without him noticing. No such luck.

"Alice Summers. May I talk to you, please?" he asks.

"I really have to go," I say.

"It will just take a moment."

I take a deep breath and turn to face him.

"I'm assuming that was not the speech that you had prepared earlier," he says. I nod. "And I'm assuming that you know that it's illegal to come to class drunk?" he says.

"I'm not drunk."

"Intoxicated, then. Either way, you can get expelled for this."

"Expelled?"

My head starts to buzz. My eyes come in and out of focus. Oh my God. What did I just do?

"I'm so sorry, Professor Milner. It will never happen again. I was just having a really bad night."

"Yes, I know that," he says with a little smile. "I heard all about it in your speech."

He's mocking me. I shake my head. Look down at the floor. I don't know what to do.

"I'm going to have to fail you on this assignment," he says.

I'm going to get kicked out of school. What am I going to do?

"But," he says, giving me hope. I look up at him. "I won't report this incident to the Dean of Students if you promise to go see an alcohol and drug abuse counselor."

"But I don't have an alcohol problem. I hardly ever drink," I say.

"You're drunk in my classroom. That's enough for me to know that something is wrong."

"Okay," I say, dropping my shoulders.

"You have to see this counselor every week for the rest of the semester. Starting this week," he says. "If you miss a meeting, I'll have no choice but to report your behavior to the Dean of Students."

"The rest of the semester?"

Professor Milner ignores me. He writes something on a piece of paper and hands it to me.

"The counselor's name is Dr. Greyson. She's very nice. Here's her office number. I'll let her know to expect your call."

Still not into you

THE BUZZ from the alcohol starts to wear off by the time I get home. Instead, it's replaced with a blistering headache. As if the day wasn't completely shitty already, it also starts to rain and I get completely soaked walking back to the dorm.

I put on a fresh pot of coffee as soon as I get in. After I change out of my wet clothes, I go back out to the kitchen and see Hudson pouring himself a cup.

"That's my coffee," I say.

"I think there's enough for two," he says with a smile.

"I don't care. I'm going to drink two cups myself. You have to make your own."

"Okay, jeez, what's wrong with you?" he says, pushing the cup toward me.

I shake my head. The Advil hasn't kicked in yet. It hurts to talk.

"I saw you," I say after I finish one cup of coffee and start on another.

He stares at me as if he doesn't know what I'm talking about.

"Yesterday, at The Martini."

"What...what were you doing there?" he asks.

I look him straight in the eyes. They twinkle in the light. Look as beautiful as always. I hate them now.

"I was talking to Juliet about how I don't see you

anymore and she suggested that we go spy on you," I say. "Who is she?"

"Nobody." He shrugs.

"Didn't look like nobody. You two looked really cozy together."

"Alice, she's nobody. Just Kathryn. I told you about her. She works with me."

"I thought you all go there together? As a group."

"Well, yesterday everyone suddenly cancelled," he says.

"How convenient," I say sarcastically.

"Listen, nothing happened," Hudson says. He puts his arm on my shoulder. I shrug him off.

"Don't touch me," I say. "How can you say nothing happened. You two were laughing the whole time. She put her hand on your leg. Then you kissed. I saw you."

He shakes his head.

"I pushed her away. Immediately. I don't like her that way. I love you."

"Doesn't feel like it," I say.

"I know that she likes me, but she's my colleague. I want to be nice. She also knows about you."

I shake my head. This conversation isn't really going as I had planned.

"I just hate being this way with you, Hudson. I hate that you're gone all the time and now I'm

Still not into you

becoming some sort of jealous, crazy girlfriend. This isn't who I am."

"I know." He nods. "I know that I work too long and I should not go out with everyone so much. There's this whole party atmosphere there. It's hard to explain."

I shrug. I understand, but I don't really hear an apology. At least, not one that I believe. Just a lot of excuses.

15

Neither of us says anything for a while. I want to tell him that I don't know how to deal with this. I know he wasn't cheating — I don't think he would, no matter what Juliet says. Even though the flirting and the interrupted kiss is as far as it will go, I still feel shitty about this. The main thing I want to tell him is to just stop. Take a break. Have a little fun. I feel like we're some sort of old married couple that are like two ships passing in the night due to their hectic work schedules. Mainly his schedule, actually. I don't say any of these things. Instead, I sit across from him and pout.

"I'm sorry, Alice," Hudson finally says. He takes my hands in his. He stares at me—I feel his gaze burning a hole in my face—until I look up. I see my reflection in his eyes. I also see someone who is at a loss as to what to do. The despondent look in his eyes frightens me.

"I don't know, Hudson." I shrug. "You really hurt me, you know? I just felt like a total idiot sitting there, watching you flirt with Kathryn."

"I wasn't flirting. We were just laughing over what someone said back in the office."

"It looked like flirting," I say. "And then when you kissed…"

Shivers run up my spine. I can't even handle saying the word.

"We didn't kiss, Alice. She kissed me. I didn't see it coming. When it happened, I pulled away right away and I told her that I have a girlfriend and it's going to stay that way. That I love you."

"I guess," I say, sighing.

"But I understand how you feel." He finally says something I want to hear. Something I'm yearning to hear. "I understand that it was awful for you. Just as it would be for me if you ever…"

Hudson lets his voice drift off. I can see that the thought of it is painful to him, too.

He comes closer to me. Takes me into his arms. This time I don't push him away. I want him close. I want to get over this. Whatever it is. I want to find a way to forgive. He lifts up my head. Slowly, Hudson presses his lips to my cheek. He gives me soft, tiny kisses as if his lips were wings of a butterfly. Cradling my face, he buries his fingers in my hair

Still not into you

and brings his lips to mine. I close my eyes and part my lips.

Hudson's lips are soft. Effervescent. His tongue inside my mouth feels like home. Like finally, we're somewhere where we belong. He drops his head and tilts mine. I feel his lips run down my neck. His kisses are so soft, the hairs on the back of my neck stand up.

Somehow, we end up in my bedroom. I have no idea where Juliet is, but I also don't particularly care. I just hope that she doesn't come home any time soon.

We fall into bed together. Our legs intertwine. His hands caress my shoulders and run down both sides of my body. As we grind against each other, we shed our clothes. My legs open and his intertwine with mine.

"Wait, I have to get my wallet," he mumbles. I nod. He needs to get a condom. We've never had unprotected sex. I've been meaning to go on the pill, but that requires going to the gynecologist. I hate doctors, let alone gynecologists, so I've been putting it off.

When Hudson's ready, he plops back next to me.

"You're so beautiful," he says, brushing hair out of my face.

"So are you," I say, smiling.

I pull him on top of me and kiss him. His hair falls into my eyes. He comes into me. Slowly, our bodies start to move in sync. His hands slide up and down my body and I bury my fingernails into his back. I start to moan with pleasure. Our bodies rise and fall with each movement.

"Oh, shit!" Hudson says and pulls out of me. "Oh my God, no, no, no."

I look down. The condom is broken.

"What does this mean?" he asks. "What are we going to do?"

I shrug. "I don't know."

"Oh my God, you can't get pregnant."

"I know! Stop freaking out," I say. "It's going to be fine. You didn't…finish yet. So, the likelihood is probably really small."

"But there's still a likelihood," he says.

"I don't know." I shrug.

We sit in bed for a few moments, staring at each other. We both know that the night is over and there is no way to recover it now. Eventually, I grab my clothes and hand Hudson his.

LATER THAT EVENING, I meet up with Hudson again in the living room. He's watching TV, but not really watching. Just flipping through the channels, looking for something to watch.

"There's nothing good on," he says.

"Yeah, I know," I say.

Hudson turns off the TV and grabs a Red Bull out of the refrigerator.

Still not into you

"Isn't it a little late for Red Bull?" I ask.

"No," he says, shaking his head. "I have a lot of Macroeconomics to do. I think I'm going to fail that class."

"I'm sure you won't."

"Can I tell you something, Alice?" he asks and continues without waiting for my answer. "I just feel a lot of pressure. I'm working these crazy hours. I don't have time for anything. Not for my classes. Not for you. Not even for work. You know, I don't really know what I'm supposed to do there. I mean, I look at those charts and figures and they just intimidate me, but I pretend that I know what's going on and that's exhausting."

"I can imagine," I sympathize.

"As for going out afterward. I often don't want to go. Really. I just want to come home and be with you and study, though I don't really want to study."

"So, why don't you?" I ask.

"Because I hear the way they all talk about other interns who didn't come along and how all the full-time people mock them for skipping out. All those people who didn't go out with them—well, they're not working there now. Tim told me that many of them are still struggling to find work six months after finishing college."

I nod. I want to sympathize. I want to say something that will make him feel better, but nothing comes to mind.

"Hudson, it's your freshman year of college. You

shouldn't be working so hard. You should have some fun."

"Alice, I'm talking to you about something serious that I'm going through and you…you just act like it's nothing. Like what I do doesn't matter. Don't you know how that makes me feel?"

I shrug. "I didn't mean it like that. I didn't want to…"

"I know. You never mean it, but that doesn't change the fact that you've said it."

I don't know what's happening here. How did all of this suddenly become my fault?

"I know you're working hard, but maybe the internship is just too much. I mean, you're going to an Ivy League school and it's your freshman year. You should be able to have some fun sometimes. You're practically entitled to it."

"And what makes me entitled to it, exactly?" he asks.

"I don't know. The fact that you're eighteen years old. If you're not going to have fun now, when are you going to?"

He shrugs. Drops his shoulders. I run over the conversation in my head. I didn't mean to get into another fight or maybe this is just a continuation of the last one. I don't know anymore.

I turn around to head back to my room. Everything is still completely unresolved, but I don't think anything will improve today. It seems to be

Still not into you

one of those things that you have to sleep on in order to get a fresh perspective.

"The thing is that, Alice, my life is just so complicated right now," Hudson says. I guess he wants to keep talking. "I'm torn in all of these directions," he adds.

"I know," I say. I come back toward him and put my hand on his shoulder. "You need to take some things off your plate. It's too crowded."

"I want to." He nods.

I look at Hudson. He looks tired but close to saying something important. Finally, he's going to make me a priority. That must be what this is all about. So just come on out with it. Say it.

"So, you understand?" he asks.

"I think so." I nod. "You're going to try to get out of the internship?"

"Get out of the internship?" he asks. "You don't really understand at all!"

"What are you talking about?"

"The internship is hard and time-consuming, but it's also super important. I can't believe that you still don't get that. I mean, how many times do I have to tell you?"

I hear anger in his voice.

"Okay, okay." I get it. "There's no need to raise your voice. You're just complaining about it so I thought…"

"So, I complain about it. So what? You're

supposed to be supportive. You're supposed to be understanding about it."

I shrug. I don't understand anything that's going on anymore.

"What I'm trying to say is that I'm a little confused with everything right now. That's why we're off. Why this is getting so complicated," Hudson says.

He gestures, pointing to us. What he means is that we're complicated. We're off, as a couple.

"I'm confused about everything," he says again.

"Stop saying that. I don't know what you mean. Say what you really mean," I say in my most insistent voice. His metaphor keeps going over my head, leaving me confused.

"I'm confused about us, Alice."

The words hang in the air as if they are suspended on a string. I stare at him. What's happening here?

"I think we need to take a break."

My ears start to buzz. Hudson keeps on talking, explaining, but I don't hear a thing. Everything turns to black.

16

I go see Dr. Greyson the next day. I want to stay in bed and never come out again, but I can't miss the appointment or I'll get kicked out of school. At this point, however, I can't even imagine graduating. Nothing else happened last night after Hudson told me that he wants to take a break from us. At least not for me. Hudson kept talking, but I don't know what he said. Eventually, I said that I had to go to bed and I haven't seen him since.

I barely have the energy to change out of my sweats, but somehow, I manage to make it to Dr. Greyson's office all the way across campus. I don't know what to expect, but I also don't stress out about it much. I've become a robot. Operating entirely on autopilot.

Unfortunately, there's no line. Dr. Greyson comes out and greets me as soon as I arrive. I take a deep breath and walk into her office. Dr. Greyson is a beautiful, no-nonsense African-American woman in her early 40s. She has gorgeous olive skin and perfectly manicured nails. Her suit looks like it's tailored and her heels look expensive—if only Juliet was here, then she'd tell me exactly how much they cost. When she asks me to sit down, her voice reminds me of Oprah's, even though Dr. Greyson is about half her size.

Her office is decorated with photos of exotic places. Tropical islands, white sandy beaches, schools of fish swirling around corals—places that seem so far away from here they might as well be on another planet.

"You like to travel?" she asks, catching me staring at one photo with 'Thailand' written underneath. The photo has a long, wind-swept palm tree coming down to earth and kissing the sand.

"I like your photos," I say. "Definitely not New York, huh?"

She nods. She doesn't say another word. It takes me a moment to realize that she's waiting for me to answer her question.

"Yes, I do," I finally say. "I haven't travelled too much, though. I really enjoy it when I do go. I hope to travel a lot more in the future."

Somewhere warm, I continue talking in my head. Somewhere with coconut palms where you don't need to wear layers of clothes to stay warm. I've never really thought of it until this very

Still not into you

moment, but clothes insulate people. You put on these layers and they separate you from the world. Make you feel as if the world isn't right there and other people aren't like you. This isn't really a complete thought yet. I don't know what I'm thinking. It just feels like that, sitting in this office, wearing a t-shirt, a sweater, jeans, boots, a scarf, and holding my jacket on my lap. It just seems like too much right now. Oh, what I wouldn't give to be in a tank top, shorts, and flip-flops right about now.

"Professor Milner has filled me in about what happened in class," Dr. Greyson says. Her voice shatters the silence of the room and brings me back to reality. I had let my mind drift off a bit.

"Yeah," I say with a nod. I don't really know what else to say about that incident.

"He told me about why you were sent here, but now I want to hear it from you."

"I know you're an alcohol abuse counselor, but I don't really drink. Not really. Not at all. I have a beer and I'm completely drunk. That's how much of a lightweight I am."

"I understand." She nods.

"So, I don't really know what I'm doing here."

"Well, you may not drink, but you did show up to class drunk and gave a drunken speech. So, you are dealing with something and I want to hear about it."

I sigh and fill her in on the details. She listens carefully. When I'm done, she nods her head.

"So, what's going on with your boyfriend, Hudson, now? It is all resolved?" she asks.

I shake my head no. Not even close.

"I don't think we're together anymore," I whisper. I feel tears start to build up at the back of my throat. *Don't cry. Don't cry.*

I take a deep breath and the tears suddenly dissipate without coming out. Thank God. The weepy feeling goes away and I just feel a little dead inside.

"Something happened last night," I say. She waits for me to continue. Not pushing me beyond the pace at which I'm comfortable. I don't know if I have the strength to say it out loud. "The condom broke," I whisper.

"What?" Dr. Greyson sits up in her chair. I don't repeat it. "Alice, when did this happen?"

"Last night."

"You need to go to the health office. You need to get the Plan B pill. It works within seventy-two hours."

I nod. I don't want to.

"I know you don't want to deal with it right now," she says urgently, "but you have to. You only have seventy-two hours. If you go to the health office, they'll give you a prescription and you can get it filled tonight."

"I don't know." I shake my head. "It's probably fine. He didn't…orgasm."

Still not into you

The word feels awful in this clinical environment, but I couldn't think of another one.

"It doesn't matter. There's still a chance that you might get pregnant. You have to take care of this."

I sigh.

"Alice, if you don't promise to take care of this, I'm going to take you to the health office myself. This is very important. Unless of course, you want to get pregnant at eighteen."

I don't. That's the last thing I want.

"Okay, I promise." I shrug.

I STAND in line at the closest drugstore, the Duane Read a few blocks away from the dorm. *Could this week get any worse?* I think to myself, perusing through *People* magazine. All of these people dressed up in the best dresses for the Golden Globes in warm Los Angeles. Oh, what I wouldn't give to be back there. I don't have to be at the Golden Globes, I just want to go home. Away from this place. Away from this week.

"Alice? Alice!" I hear someone calling my name. I don't recognize the voice. I don't want to talk to anyone right now. Shit.

When I turn around, I come face-to-face with Tea and let out a sigh. Tea is one of the best people to run into.

"What are you doing here?" she asks.

"Just getting some medication. You?"

"Me, too. Well, not medication, but I have to pick up a few things."

They call my name. The pharmacist gives me the box and instructs me about how to use it. I nod and pay the amount. $70! Crap. Why the hell is it so expensive? The pharmacist asks me about insurance, but I say I don't have any. It's a lie. I do have some but it's through my parents' and I don't want them to find out.

"Oh my God, Alice," Tea says. "I couldn't help but overhear. Plan B. Are you okay?"

I shrug. "I'll be fine."

I didn't plan on telling her what happened with Hudson, but it just comes out. In the hosiery aisle, of all places. Right in front of a wall of leggings.

"I can't believe that you two broke up." Tea shakes her head. "I'm so sorry. And now you have to deal with this on top of all that?"

I sigh. I have to attend mandatory alcohol abuse counseling too. I still don't know how the hell I'm going to pass my public speaking class at this point. Tea asks me if I want to have a cup of coffee next door. That sounds like a great idea.

"Hey, you know what you need?" she asks as we share a croissant. I take a sip of my coffee. "Why don't you come to Atlantic City with us?"

"What?"

"Tanner and I are going to Atlantic City this weekend. I'd love for you to come."

Still not into you

"No, no, you guys are going on a romantic getaway…" I start to say.

"Well, it is Valentine's Day, but it's not like that."

Valentine's Day. Oh my God. That's right! It's this weekend. I had completely forgotten about it.

"What do you mean?" I ask.

"I have to go there to research something for this book I'm writing. Tanner is coming along. It's too soon for us to go on a weekend trip. So actually, you'll be doing me a favor if you come."

"I don't know," I say. "I don't want to be a third wheel. I'm sure that Tanner wants some romantic time with you on Valentine's Day."

"Okay, well, then invite some people. I'd love to have extra people there."

"Tea, what's wrong? Are you not that into Tanner?"

She sighs. "No, I am. I'm just…I don't really want to go away for a weekend with him. I'm not ready to sleep with him yet."

"Oh," I say. "Oh, I see. If you two go away together, share a hotel room…then you think…"

"Exactly," she says. "So, you're really going to be doing me a favor. Invite your roommates, too. The more, the merrier. Juliet. Dylan. Maybe not Hudson."

"Ha, yeah, probably not Hudson." I smile. "I guess a trip away from here does sound nice."

"Excellent, then it's decided!" She grins from ear to ear.

"So, tell me about this book. That's exciting!" I say. "Was it what you were working on before? About Belize?"

"No." She shakes her head. "It's a completely different story. It's actually a romance novel."

"Really? Wow."

"I know. I never thought I'd write one, but then I read a few and they're really exciting and passionate. I just wanted to try my hand at it."

"So, what's it about?" I ask.

"I'm not entirely set on the name yet," Tea says. "It's either going to be called *A Weeklong Fiancé* or *Fiancé for a Week*."

"Hmm, I'm intrigued."

"It's about this normal girl. She's a copywriter at an online magazine. Just graduated from college. She has an apartment, a roommate, and an unhealthy obsession with chocolate and shoes."

"Well, who doesn't, right?" I say with a wink.

"She's drowning in student loans, has no idea how she's going to pay them off. Then she gets an offer that's too good to pass up. Take a weeklong cruise to the Caribbean with a dashing, rich stranger and pretend to be his fiancée at his family reunion. For $10,000. No sex. Business only."

"Wow, seems like most girls would do it for way less than that."

"That's what she thinks. Then she starts to fall in love with him," Tea says.

"I love it!" I say. I do. Really.

Still not into you

"So, this trip to Atlantic City is a little bit of a research trip. I've never been to a casino before and I want to get a taste of what it's like. What it looks like, etc."

"I get it." I nod. "I'd love to read your book when you're done."

"You'll be the first."

17

There was no way I was going to go on this trip without at least Juliet. I was excited when Dylan decided to come along, too. They don't know Tea very well, and none of us have ever met Tanner, but they were down for a fun weekend. When I first told Dylan about this, he invited Hudson as well, but luckily for me, Hudson said that he had too much work to do. Peyton was invited, too, and she was planning on coming along until she remembered that she had a big paper due on Monday.

Juliet, Dylan, and I are sharing an Uber to Grand Central Station. Juliet and I over-packed a little and we're laden down with bags that wouldn't fit in the trunk.

"Why did you two have to pack so much?" Dylan asks. He only packed one small suitcase, the size of a carry-on. "It's just two nights."

"You wouldn't understand," Juliet rolls her eyes.

"Just pack a couple of outfits and that should be enough," Dylan insists.

"What happens when you don't feel like wearing one? Or it's inappropriate to wear it? No, you have to have backups."

I didn't pack as much as Juliet, but I definitely took too much. There seems to always be shirts and pants that you think you might wear, that you almost should wear, but for some reason never do.

"So, what's going on with you and Hudson?" Dylan turns to me.

Juliet makes a face at him as if to ask why the hell he's bringing him up.

"Sorry, I didn't mean to make you uncomfortable. It just seems that something's off, but Hudson didn't tell me what exactly."

I shrug.

Hudson and I haven't spoken much since that night. Though he did corner me by the bathroom this morning and insisted on talking.

"Alice, I just want you to know that I don't want to break up," he said. "That's the last thing I want."

"You don't want to break up? I thought that was exactly what you wanted."

"No, not at all. I just want to take a break. A breather."

"That sounds like a breakup."

"No, not at all," he said.

"And what's the difference?" I asked.

Still not into you

"I just need a little time. A little space, but I want to be with you. I don't want to be with anyone else and I hope you don't either."

"So, I'm just supposed to wait around for you? Is that right?"

"Look, the way I see this break is just that. A break. I'm not going to date anyone and I hope you don't either. I'm just confused and I need time to get myself back together."

"Alice?" Dylan asks. "You okay?"

"Huh? What?" I ask.

"You seemed to have spaced out a bit."

"Oh, right, sorry. I don't know what to say about Hudson. I don't know what's going on."

"Wait, are you two back together?" Juliet asks.

"No, definitely not. Apparently, according to him, we were never broken up. Just on a break. Whatever the hell that means," I say.

We ride the rest of the way to Grand Central in silence. My mind drifts back to Hudson, unwillingly. I still don't completely understand the difference between a break and a breakup, nor do I really care. I'm not sure if I'm down to be on this break, whatever it is. All I know is that I'm looking forward to going on this trip and forgetting all about Hudson and everything that has happened this weekend. I need to dance, drink a little too much, and let go of all this crap.

THE THREE OF us meet up with Tea and Tanner inside Grand Central. As we walk toward them, I smile at the fact that all the girls seemed to have over-packed and both of the guys under-packed. Tea makes all the introductions as soon as we come up.

Tanner is definitely hot. He's about 6'4" with gorgeous eyes and lustrous hair. His dark hair matches his dark eyes and his five o'clock shadow makes him look mysterious. He's three years older than Dylan. While Dylan often comes off cocky, Tanner seems confident and self-assured. Perhaps it's something that Dylan will grow into in time.

Tanner and Tea make a cute couple. He helps her with her bags on the way to the train and gives her a peck on the top of her head as we wait. I'm suddenly really thankful that Peyton decided not to come. They're the only couple here and the balance of power is definitely on the singles. It would not be the case if Peyton were here.

Everyone gets to know each other during the two-and-a-half-hour train ride to Atlantic City and it feels like we're old friends by the time we arrive in the hotel suite that Tea and Tanner got for our stay.

Still not into you

"Are you sure you two don't want us to get our own hotel room?" Juliet asks.

"No, of course not," Tea says a little too fast. I notice that Tanner isn't so quick to vote for everyone staying at the suite. "That's why we got the suite. So there would be room for everyone."

Well, almost everyone. The plan is that Tea and Tanner get the bedroom, which is separated from the living room by two French doors, and the three of us sleep on the couches in the living room. There are two long couches, for Juliet and I, and Dylan will sleep on the floor.

"As long as I'm not the one sleeping on the floor, I'm fine," Juliet announces and starts to unpack her bag.

"This is going to be a fun night," Juliet says in front of the bathroom mirror.

The three of us cram ourselves into the bathroom and share it. Unfortunately, there are only two plugs—one short of how many we need. Tea is blow-drying her hair and I'm flat-ironing my hair. Juliet, who's planning on curling hers, waits patiently for her turn while applying false lashes.

Both Tea and Juliet came on this trip prepared. Not just in terms of the clothes they had packed, but also with their makeup kits. Juliet's makeup bag can be a whole separate carry-on bag. Tea's isn't so big, but it unfolds, and once it's all unfolded, it puts mine to shame.

I only packed a small Ziploc bag of what I'd need. Now, I'm starting to think that I need a lot of more. After Juliet and Tea unpack their supplies on the counter, it looks like the backstage of a Victoria Secret show. They both have so many tools and brushes that I don't even know what they're all for.

"So, you know they have eyebrow extensions now, right?" Juliet asks Tea.

"Yes, I know. I saw it on Instagram. Aren't they amazing?" Tea asks.

"I'd love to get some. I think I over-plucked mine a little bit in high school."

They both stare at their eyebrows in the mirror. I'm suddenly become super self-conscious of my own eyebrows. Perhaps they're not up to snuff.

"Well, not everyone can have naturally beautiful brows like Alice," Tea adds.

"I know, right? They're amazing!"

I roll my eyes. "A few years ago, they were too bushy, but now they're apparently just right."

"Well, a few years ago, everyone was wearing low-rise jeans and showing their hip bones and now it's all about high rise," Juliet says.

"Yeah, that's the cool thing about fashion. It changes all the time," Tea adds.

"That's also the stressful thing about fashion," I add. "It changes all the time."

I free up one plug for Juliet to plug her curling

Still not into you

iron into and go to the living room. I don't contour my face—just put on some foundation, eyeliner, mascara, eye shadow, and lipstick. That's enough for me.

There's a knock at the door. When I open it, I see Tanner with a bag of alcohol and a case of beer. Since he's the only one of us who can legally drink, he was sent out to get everything for the pre-game.

"Pre-gaming is about to commence!" Dylan announces.

Pre-gaming is a very important tradition in college. Since most of us aren't legally able to buy drinks, we use the time before we go out to get a little drunk. Plus, the drinks are way cheaper this way. Dylan asks everyone what they want. I ask for a martini. Forty-five minutes later, just when we're all ready to leave and I'm finally done with it, I'm already feeling like I had a little bit too much. Unfortunately, I keep drinking.

18

I open my eyes. My head is pounding as if someone is smashing on drums with all their might a millimeter away from my eardrums. A sliver of light peeks in through the blackout curtains and my eyes can barely handle it.

"Oh my God," I whisper. My throat itches. I cough and feel the nightstand for something to drink. My hand lands on a glass. I bring it to my lips and then take a sniff.

Please don't be alcohol, I say to myself. It's not. Just water. Whew. I drink the whole glass. Finally, I manage to open my eyes a little wider. The room is pretty dark, but the light still pierces my eyes as if it's a sword. I cover my eyes with my arm and look around.

Where the hell am I?

I'm sitting in a tall bed. There are suitcases all

around. And French doors across from me. The place does not look familiar, however.

My eyes dart to one side and I spot the bathroom. Carefully, I get up and walk to the bathroom. I don't put on the lights, but I do look at myself in the mirror. I'm a mess. Not even a hot mess. My hair is completely out of place. Crumpled and sad. My makeup is all smeared and I have ugly raccoon eyes. I wipe my mouth—lipstick residue comes off on the back of my hand.

"Where is this?" I whisper.

My eyes adjust to the muted light enough for me to stop protecting them with my hand. I look around the bathroom. It's familiar and foreign at the same time. I feel like I've been here before, but not often. This is not our bathroom back at the dorm. Then I see it. My tiny, bright pink, travel-sized flat iron. It hits me. I'm at the hotel. We're in Atlantic City. For some reason I'm in the room. Weren't Tea and Tanner supposed to sleep here?

I come back into the room. What the hell am I doing sleeping here and everyone else sleeping there? I search my mind for answers, but it all comes up blank. I can't remember a thing.

"Oh, shit, why is it so bright in here?" I hear someone say.

The voice startles me. It's quiet, but it's definitely not coming from the outside.

It's coming from the bed.

Please don't be Tanner.

Still not into you

Please don't be Tanner.

Please don't be Tanner.

When he moves the cover from his face and sits up in bed, I see that it's not Tanner.

It's Dylan.

"Dylan? What are you doing here?" I ask.

"Stop yelling! My head is killing me."

I give him a moment to collect his thoughts. He gets up and pulls the blackout shades shut. The sliver of light is gone. My head feels a little better.

"What are you wearing?" Dylan asks me.

I don't know. I didn't even think to look. I look down. For some reason, I'm wearing a white bathing suit cover-up. It's light and airy and has tiny little spaghetti straps.

"I don't know," I say, shrugging. What I don't reveal is that I'm also not wearing underwear.

Dylan sits up more in bed. He's not wearing a shirt either.

"Are you wearing any clothes?" I ask him, cautiously.

He rubs the back of his head. Then looks down.

"No." He shakes his head. He acts like it's no big deal. Just gives out a little sigh. Clearly, he's not fully understanding the magnitude of this situation.

"Oh, shit," I say. "Do you think we…?"

I can't finish the sentence. No, we couldn't have. Right? I try to remember something, anything, from last night. Why did I have to drink so much? The last thing I remember is staggering up some stairs at a casino (which one?) with Juliet. My phone said it was 1:30 a.m. or maybe 3:30 a.m.? I have no idea.

"Do you think we what?" Dylan asks.

His mind isn't working well. Either that or he's particularly dense.

"I'm not wearing underwear," I decide to inform him, "and you're naked."

"Oh, shit," he whispers. The expression on his face says it all. Peyton. They just got back together. This is Valentine's Day, for crying out loud.

"I can't remember anything," he says.

"Me neither." I shake my head.

"You can't tell Peyton about this. Promise me that you won't. She'll never forgive me."

I nod.

"No, you have to promise," he says. He's speaking really fast. It sounds like he's about to hyperventilate.

"I promise. I don't want Hudson to know either," I say.

Oh my God, Hudson! This is the first time he has popped into my head this whole morning.

"Oh, wow, Hudson," Dylan mumbles. They are roommates and really good friends. This doesn't look right, not at all. "Maybe nothing happened," Dylan says. "I mean, we don't remember a thing. So maybe we were too drunk."

"Yeah, maybe," I mumble. "I hope you're right."

I find my underwear under the bed and put it

Still not into you

on. I turn around as Dylan puts on his clothes. I don't want to tell him this, but this is going to be a hard one to hide. Juliet is outside and she's our roommate and not just our roommate, Hudson's roommate. If we did sleep together, the news is just too juicy for her to keep quiet. If Hudson finds out, I'm sure that Peyton will, too. He won't be in a very forgiving mood. Besides, I'm not even sure if I want to keep it from Hudson. We're not really together anymore.

Dylan and I walk out of the room with hung heads. I'm actually tiptoeing. I hope that everyone is still asleep. Unfortunately, they're not. There's a room service cart in the middle of the room and everyone's having breakfast.

"Wow, look who's up!" Juliet announces to the whole room. Tanner stops pouring his cup of coffee. Tea looks up from her magazine.

"Hey." I smile and wave. "Morning."

Without saying a word, I walk over to the open box of donuts and grab one with cherry filling spilling out of its side. Sugar isn't the best way to start the day, but I need a pick-me-up. A big one.

"So…how does it feel?" Tea asks.

Dylan and I look at each other. He has a confused look on his face. I'm equally perplexed.

"What?" he asks.

Okay, so maybe we had slept together, even though neither of us remembers. How is this their business exactly? It's not, but it doesn't stop them from gossiping. I hate to admit it, but if Dylan and Tea slept together, I'd be all over it as well.

"I can't believe you two did that last night." Tea shakes her head. She has a mischievous smile on her face.

"We don't remember a thing," I finally admit. "Why were we sleeping in that room anyway? Wasn't that supposed to be your room?"

"Yes, but after what happened…we just thought it would be more appropriate," Tea says with a shrug.

Why is she being so mysterious?

"What happened?" I ask. I search all of my memories from last night in an effort to find one that would explain this, but nothing comes to mind.

"Wait a second!" Juliet says, getting excited. Her eyes light up and she gets a big grin on her face. "Wait a second!"

I hate how dramatic she can be sometimes. How animated.

"Are you two *really*, and I mean *really*, telling us that you don't remember what happened last night?"

Dylan and I exchange looks. We both shrug and shake our heads.

"No," I mumble. "Not really."

Still not into you

"What's the last thing you remember?" Juliet asks.

"Um," I say. "Walking around the casino, going up some stairs somewhere, drinking. A lot."

"And you?" Juliet turns to Dylan.

"Not much else," he says. "I don't even remember going up any stairs."

"Oh. My. God!" Juliet shrieks and jumps up and down. "Oh. My. God!"

"What?" I ask. "What's going on?"

Tea joins in Juliet's excitement, but Tanner just stands back a little. He doesn't shriek or jump, but he does flash me a smile. Clearly, our lack of memory is bringing everyone a great deal of joy.

"Oh, c'mon, just tell us. What happened?" Dylan says, grabbing a bagel. He starts lathering it with a generous amount of cream cheese. "What's the big deal?"

"Okay, okay," Juliet says, taking a big sigh. She's trying to calm herself down. We wait. "Okay. I can do this," she says and then bursts out laughing.

"C'mon!" I say. I'm losing my patience and I'm not really in the mood anyway. It's way too bright in this room. My head is pounding. My mouth is dry. I'm already regretting eating half the donut, even though I continue to take additional bites.

"Okay," Juliet says. "You know what you did last night?"

"No!" Dylan and I say in unison. We're both

growing more and more impatient with every second.

"Well, let me tell you," she says, clearly milking the moment. She should be an actress, I decide. She has epic timing. "What you two did last night was… get married!"

Dylan drops his bagel to the floor. It falls with the cream cheese side down. I start to choke and cough. Tea hands me a cup of water. I manage to get a few sips in.

"What?" I ask when I finally get some air. "What?"

"You got married," Juliet says again. Quietly this time. The tone of her voice is serious, but it feels like a joke.

"What do you mean?" I ask. "No, that can't be. We didn't actually get married. It was just a joke. Please, tell me it's a joke."

While I have the tendency to talk and say everything that comes to mind in times of stress, Dylan, apparently, has a completely different tendency. I turn to him for some support in this, but he just stares at the wall. As if he's frozen. Like a statue.

"Dylan." I pull on his shirt. "We didn't get married. Right?"

A moment later, he comes back to reality.

"No, we couldn't have," he whispers.

"Well, you did," Juliet says. Her certainty frightens me.

Still not into you

Tea comes over to me. She puts her arm around my shoulder.

"You did, honey," she says sympathetically.

"No, no, no." I shake my head.

"The reason you're wearing that dress," Tea says, "is that you wanted to get married in white. So, when Dylan asked you to marry him, and you said yes, we all went to the only place that was open in the casino and bought it."

"But this is a bathing suit cover-up!"

"I know. It was a resort wear store. That was all they had," Tea says.

"Look at your left hand," Juliet says.

When I look down, I see a large diamond ring. It's gorgeous.

"What is that?" Dylan comes over and takes my hand.

"You got it for her," Juliet says. "Alice thought it would be funny to get one of those lollypop rings and have that be her engagement ring, but you said that no wife of yours is going to have a lollypop ring. So, you marched into Tiffany's and got her that one and half carat diamond."

"Shit." Dylan shakes his head.

"How did this happen?" I whisper. He shrugs. "I mean, how did we even get engaged, let alone get married? Why didn't you stop us?"

All three of them look down at the floor.

"We were all drinking a lot," Tea says, "and I guess it sounded like fun."

"Fun?" I ask.

"It just felt like we were in a movie or something. I mean, that's what people do in movies, not in real life," Juliet says.

"So, what happened? How did this happen exactly?" Dylan asks.

"We were all drinking a lot," Juliet says, "and suddenly you started to complain about Peyton, or was it Alice who was complaining about Hudson?"

"I think Alice started first and then Dylan joined in," Tea says. Clearly, their memory isn't that great on all this either.

"Either way, you two were moaning about your significant others. Then Tanner said that you two would make a good couple."

"Tanner?" I ask.

"Well, I don't know you two well and I was drinking a lot."

"It was just a joke," Tea says, "but Dylan thought it was a really good idea. He started going on and on about how you two are friends and friends make the best couples. At first, you thought it was pretty funny. I went to the bathroom and came back and you two were engaged."

"Holy shit," I whisper.

19

Then suddenly, it all starts to come back to me. Not everything, but big chunks of it. I remember sitting next to Dylan, eating sushi. I got some extra soy sauce around my mouth and he wiped it away with his finger. The moment lasted a little bit too long. I didn't want it to stop. He leaned closer and kissed me. I kissed him back.

"You're such a good kisser," I said.

"So are you," he said.

"I sort of wish we could kiss longer," I joked. Then he kissed me again. This time it was longer than a kiss. It was more like a make-out session.

I don't know how much time passed, but when we stopped, he said, "I wish I could kiss you forever."

"Me, too," I mumbled.

He looked over my shoulder and smiled.

"There's a wedding chapel over there," Dylan said. "Do you think that's a sign?"

I shrugged. "Probably not."

"Well, let's make it one," he said. "Alice Summers, will you marry me?"

"Are you insane?" I asked, laughing. "Don't joke about that."

"I'm not joking. I like you. You like me. We're really good at kissing. We'll probably be even better at the other stuff."

"That's not a reason to get married!" I said.

"Of course it is! We're really good friends and relationships are complicated. So why don't we just marry each other?"

"Because we're still in college!"

"So? Wouldn't it be romantic?"

Insane and crazy, but romantic? Yes, I guessed so.

"Besides, Hudson would hate it," Dylan added.

Well, if he would hate it then… I started to waver.

"C'mon, say yes. Please say yes," he said and kissed me again. When we pulled away this time, we were engaged.

"This can't be happening," I say. Everyone's staring at us.

"You're remembering it, right? I can see that,"

Still not into you

Juliet says. I nod and drop my shoulders. "Dylan? How about you?" Juliet asks.

"Bits and pieces," he whispers.

"Well, here's your signed marriage certificate in case you forget again," Juliet says, handing us the paper. "The minister said that you should expect to get something in the mail about it as well."

I have to sit down. My head hasn't stopped throbbing and the locomotive whistling and banging around up there now seemed to have picked up speed. I have no idea what to do about this. All I know is that I don't want anyone to find out about it. This is so embarrassing. So humiliating. So not like me. I don't get drunk and do crazy things like this. I'm just a regular person.

This is all Hudson's fault. If he hadn't wanted us to take a break, I would never have been here alone complaining to Dylan about this. I wouldn't have ever even kissed him, let alone married him.

Oh my God! My breaths get shallow. My heart starts to beat faster. What if Hudson finds out? He can't find out. Ever. If he does, it will crush him. This will definitely change our status from a break to a breakup. I don't want to break up.

My mind's racing. I don't know how to stop it. I need to lie down.

DYLAN and I ride the train back to school in silence.

Neither of us is in the mood to talk. The train's not too crowded and there's enough room for both of us to take up entire seats. I sit across from him in the window seat. Juliet, Tea, and Tanner are planning on taking a later train, but are also coming back today. No one's really in the mood to stay too long in Atlantic City after the night we've all had.

Around Elizabeth, New Jersey, my headache finally starts to fade and I can think clearer. When I look across the aisle, I see that Dylan also stopped staring out of the window like he's unconscious.

"How could we let this happen?" I ask, sitting down in the seat next to him. He shrugs and hangs his head. "What are you going to do?" I ask. "Are you going to tell Peyton?"

"I have no idea," he whispers. "We were just getting back into this really good spot. Not fighting so much. I thought we were finally over all that bullshit from last semester. Now this…it's going to crush her."

I sigh. "I don't know what to do either," I say.

Suddenly, a look of shock and horror appears on his face.

"What's wrong?" I ask.

"You're not actually thinking of telling Hudson, are you?" he asks.

I shrug.

"Alice, you can't!" His voice aches from desperation.

I haven't actually given this any thought. Don't

get me wrong, I don't want Hudson to know. I don't want him to know any of this. I want us to go back to the way things were before he got "confused" and we went "on break". I want us to be back in that happy place where everything felt safe and I thought our love would last forever, but we're not there anymore. This weekend definitely made things a whole lot more complicated. Even though I don't want Hudson to know about what happened, I mainly want it to never have happened. I'm not sure if I want to lie to him.

"Alice?" Dylan shakes me. I must've spaced out for a moment, or ten.

"Yeah?" I ask.

My eyes focus on the earnest look on Dylan's face. He doesn't want me to say anything to Hudson and he's holding his breath, waiting for my answer.

"Alice, you can't tell him," he says.

"Why?"

"Because he's my roommate! How are we going to make it through the rest of the semester after this?"

"Wouldn't it be worse if he finds out anyway?" I ask. I can't lie; the thought of keeping this from Hudson does give me some relief.

"He won't, if you don't say anything."

"What about keeping this lie? Isn't that bad, too?"

Dylan sighs. "Of course it is, but…I just don't know any other way around it."

We don't say anything for a few minutes while we both think about this. More time doesn't really help me decide either way.

"Okay, what about this?" Dylan says, turning to me. "What if we first try to get this whole thing resolved? You know, get un-married. Then, and only then, tell him the truth."

That actually sounds like a good idea. Wow, I'm impressed.

"Yeah, that sounds like it could work," I say. "And by un-married, you mean…"

"I don't know, I guess we can try to get an annulment. If that doesn't work out, then maybe a…divorce."

That word. Divorce. It sounds so adult. Even more than married. Lots of people get married. Not everyone gets divorced. Especially at nineteen.

"Wow, divorce," I say, trying to come to grips with the foreignness of the word. "I always thought that I'd have a house with wall-to-wall carpeting, a big mortgage, a golden retriever, and an SUV before I'd ever do that."

"I thought those things were a requirement," Dylan says, flashing me a smile. I laugh. This is the first time we've smiled since last night. It feels good to do it again.

"So, you think we can get an annulment instead? What is that exactly?" I ask.

An annulment sounds more reasonable than a divorce. I mean, we were really drunk. This was a

Still not into you

mistake. How can our situation be subject to the same thing as people who have been married for years? Shouldn't there be some sort of special clause for accidental weddings?

"I don't really know," Dylan says with a shrug. "From what I've seen on TV, I think it's some sort of alternative divorce for people who were coerced into marriage."

"Hmm, well, maybe we were coerced. We drank too much. We can't be held responsible for this," I say.

"I'm not sure it works that way." He nods. "This is Atlantic City. If everyone said that they were drunk and should get the opportunity to get a do-over, none of the casinos would be in business anymore."

"I guess not," I say.

"As soon as we're back, I'm going to find out exactly what an annulment is and whether we can get it instead of a divorce," Dylan says. "But before we do that, we have to make a promise to each other."

"Didn't we already do that?" I joke. "Promised to love each other through thick and thin? For richer and poorer?"

Dylan cracks a smile.

"Look where that got us," he says. "Okay, let's promise each other that we're not going to tell anyone about this. I mean not anyone. Not Hudson. Not Peyton. Not even friends back home. Until this is all resolved."

I look straight into his eyes. They twinkle under the harsh fluorescent lights.

"I promise," I say with a nod.

"I promise, too," Dylan says. For a second, we dance around possibly giving each other a brief hug to solidify the promise. Instead, we settle on a handshake. It's more professional. Less intimate.

"Oh, and don't forget to text Juliet and Tea and Tanner and tell them what we've decided. We can't have Hudson and Peyton finding out any of this by accident," Dylan says.

I nod and get my phone.

20

I arrive at Dr. Greyson's office on a cold February day. The clouds hang low in the sky and the world is so gray and colorless, it feels like it's in mourning. The trees on campus stand stark naked, without a leaf in sight. It is on days like these that I miss the sunshine of Southern California the most. I miss the mountains and the endless blue sky. I try to remember what it's like to not feel claustrophobic all the time—from both the tall buildings and the low sky, but I can't. It has been more than a month since I've been home and a month of clouds and grayness makes it hard to remember anything. Sitting in Dr. Greyson's waiting room, I wonder if I can even make it here four years.

"I feel like this weather is making everything in my life worse," I complain to Dr. Greyson.

She's wearing a gray pantsuit and black heels. I

glance down at her feet. A little bit of her olive skin is exposed between the end of her shoe and her pant leg. It's barely twenty degrees out and I wonder if she wears these shoes outside or if she has boots or sneakers hiding somewhere underneath her desk, which she changes into on her way home.

"What do you mean?" Dr. Greyson asks.

"It's just so cold and gray. It has been like this for more than a week and it just makes me so depressed. I don't know if I can live here for four years."

"Well, February does tend to be the coldest month. Luckily, it's also the shortest month," Dr. Greyson says.

I look at her. There's an unusual amount of pep and optimism in her voice, but it quickly disappears when she finally realizes what I'm really saying.

"Are you trying to tell me something, Alice?" she asks, pursing her bright red lips. They are large and perfectly lined. I wonder how she gets her lipstick to stick the whole time. If I wear lipstick to one of these sessions, it's usually completely gone by the end, but hers remains intact, bright and perfect, as if she had just applied it.

"I don't know." I shrug. "It's just something I've been thinking of recently."

"What?"

"Transferring."

"Transferring out of Columbia? To go where?" Dr. Greyson asks.

Still not into you

"I don't know yet. I was sort of thinking of University of Southern California. I got in there before. It's back in LA. It's warm there. My parents live there."

Dr. Greyson shakes her head. "This isn't just about the weather, is it?" she asks.

"Well, sort of. I mean, it's hardly ever gray and bleak like this there and it's never this cold. Maybe I'd have a better perspective about everything if I went there."

"Perhaps." Dr. Greyson shrugs. "But I don't want you to discount everything that you have been through recently. That takes a toll."

Ah, everything. That's one way of putting it. I don't say anything for a while.

"So, you haven't told me how you're feeling about this. Your marriage to Dylan?"

"Accidental marriage," I correct her. The accident part is supposed to make me feel better about this, like it's not all my fault. Even though I know it is.

"Okay, accidental marriage."

"I don't know how to feel about it. I just feel lost. We got back last night and Hudson was there in the living room and I felt like such a liar."

"Why?"

"Because we were hanging out and we were both acting like his friends, but we're not. Friends don't do this to friends. They don't get married and not tell him. Friends don't marry your roommate and not tell you. Friends don't marry your girlfriend and not tell you. We're both such frauds."

"It must be difficult," Dr. Greyson says.

"On top of all that, we're still technically on a break. What I mean is that we're not broken up and now I'm married to his roommate. I just don't know what to do. I need to get out of this marriage as soon as possible."

"When is that happening?"

"I don't know exactly, but soon. Dylan's looking into getting an annulment. I really hope we can do that."

I hate to admit it, but it's actually kind of nice to come and talk to Dr. Greyson. Juliet always has some sort of jokes or witty comments to offer, but Dr. Greyson is an unbiased third party. She never makes fun of me or mocks the situation, no matter how absurd. She simply listens and nods. I do, however, wish that she offered a little bit more advice. When I first started coming here, I thought she would. I've never been to therapy and I thought that she would give me the right answer and send me on my way. She doesn't. About the only thing that she does is give me one or two cryptic little sayings that could mean a number of things, but it doesn't really amount to any actual advice since they often require me to think about what I've done even more (and that leaves me even more confused about the whole thing).

Still not into you

"What about your parents?" she suddenly asks out of the blue.

"What about them?"

"Are you going to tell them about Dylan?"

"No! Absolutely not." I stare at her as if she had lost her mind. "They'd freak out and besides, I don't want anyone to find out about this. If I could not tell Hudson about this at all, it would be even better."

"But you just told me a few minutes ago that you want to tell him. That you feel like a fraud by keeping this from him."

I shake my head. "I don't know what I want. I want to just turn back time and have none of this happen."

"We all want that sometime, Alice, but unfortunately, we can't have that."

We don't speak for close to a minute. This hour is really dragging by. I sigh. Only fifteen more minutes, I say to myself.

"What are your thoughts about Public Speaking class?" she asks. "Do you have any concerns about that?"

"Concerns? Yes, you can call it that. I would say that it's more like I'm terrified and hopeless about the whole thing," I say.

"What do you mean?"

"Dylan showed me a way I could get through the speeches and I was really happy about that. I even got a B+ on the first speech, which is like a miracle, but now that my old strategy won't work anymore…" I say with a sigh.

"Alice, I wouldn't call drinking before class a strategy," Dr. Greyson says, flashing a smile.

"Why? I would." I shrug. "It was the only thing that calmed my nerves. Now I have no idea how I'm going to get through the next one. Which, by the way, is in two weeks."

"I'm going to give you a pamphlet about this next time you come in," Dr. Greyson says. "It will have a list of actual strategies for dealing with stage fright."

I shrug. "Okay," I say. I don't have my hopes up. I've read a lot of things about it on the Internet and none of them have been particularly helpful.

"You know, of course, that you can't drink again, right?" Dr. Greyson asks at the end of our meeting.

"Yes, of course." I roll my eyes. "I'll get kicked out of school for sure. Unfortunately, I think I'm going to fail that class either way."

"No, you won't," Dr. Greyson insists. She seems so certain about it, but I'm not sure. In fact, I'm pretty sure that I will fail. What else can happen if you stand up there without saying a word?

I walk out of her office and back into the cold bleakness outside. This semester was supposed to go differently. It was supposed to be fun and exciting. Hudson and I were supposed to be together. We were supposed to actually take advantage of everything that college and New York City have to offer. So why did it all go so terribly wrong?

I decide to walk through Riverside Park to clear my head. I've been dwelling on this for far too long and I know that I'm nowhere close to being done. Juliet will come home tonight wanting to talk about this weekend, wanting to offer her advice over the whole thing without really telling me anything I don't already know. Then Tea will call, I'm sure. I haven't talked to her at all since all of this happened except for one or two texts asking her to keep this weekend to herself. Then, of course, there is Hudson. He has texted me a number of times since the weekend, trying to set up a time to talk. He wants to talk about our break and I don't want to. I don't think I can face him. I mean, I don't think I can face him and keep this weekend to myself, but, at the same time, I also can't tell him what happened. It will crush him and us. Our break will definitely become a breakup. Then what? Will it mean that we're really over? That there's no more Alice and Hudson?

No, that is not how this semester was supposed to go. I walk past a couple kissing on a bench in Riverside Park. They are wrapped up in each other's kisses. Their hands are intertwined and their legs are pressed closely together. That was supposed to be us. We were supposed to be sitting on that bench and kissing, not caring that it's nearly fifteen degrees outside.

21

I've managed to avoid Hudson for a whole week. I thought it would be hard, but it wasn't. His work schedule has remained pretty much the same since our fight. He works late Monday through Wednesday and has classes all day Thursday and Friday. A couple of days, he came home way after eleven and left before I was up.

On Thursday, in Victorian Literature, I space out for nearly the whole lecture thinking about him and Kathryn. Why does she have to be so hot and so nice? I've never felt this way before. I never thought of myself as a particularly jealous person, but thinking about him and her working late at night at the office makes my skin crawl. I know we're not together anymore. Worse yet, I'm married and he doesn't even know it, but still. I don't want him to be around her, but there's nothing I can do about it.

I stay out late this evening. I know he won't be home and I just don't feel like sitting around my dorm room all day, staring at the walls or reading a million BuzzFeed articles and making extra boards to pin more curious but completely unimportant things on Pinterest.

I stop by the coffee shop that Tea and I frequent often and order a cup of green tea.

"Hey!" I hear a familiar voice.

"Hi, Hudson," I say, turning around and forcing myself to smile. What the hell is he doing here?

"What are you doing here?" he asks.

"Just getting some tea and you?"

"My class got cancelled. So, I thought I'd waste some time here," he says with a shrug. "Oh, man, I haven't seen you in forever!"

Hudson puts his arms around me. His body feels warm and firm, comforting. For a moment, I'm transported to another time. When we were still together and in love. When everything in the world was right and nothing could break us up.

"You smell so nice," he whispers, giving me a chaste peck on the cheek.

He leans over to kiss my lips, but I turn my head away. I move away from him. My whole body tenses when he puts his arm on the small of my back and doesn't remove it. Eventually, I just take a step to the side to get myself some space.

"Listen, I'm glad you're here," he says.

His face looks serious. Hudson furrows his brows

Still not into you

and his eyes look earnest and under control. It's as if he can stop them from twinkling just by willing them so.

"I can't stay," I say.

"Alice, please." Hudson takes my hand. "I feel like we've gotten off on the wrong foot. I haven't seen you much since…that happened. I really need to talk."

"No, I really can't." I shake my head and turn to leave.

"You don't have any more classes today, Alice. You're just avoiding me," he says. The desperation in his voice makes me sick to my stomach. Against my better judgement, I turn around and sit down across from him.

"Thank you," he says, picking up my hand and kissing the back of it. As if he's some sort of servant. As if I'm some sort of princess.

"What do you want to talk about?" I ask. My voice is distant and austere. I'm trying to make it as impersonal as possible. As if that can save me.

"Us," he says. This time, his eyes twinkle. The light washes over my body as if it's my conscience making me feel even more horrible than I already do. I wait for him to continue. I'm afraid that I'm going to start crying if I utter even a word. My throat closes up from the pain and my mouth runs dry.

"I'm so, so sorry about everything that happened, Alice," Hudson says. He takes my hands in his and looks me straight in the eye. At first, I try to resist, but I can't avoid his eye contact no matter where I turn. He forces me to lock eyes with him.

"I was a real asshole," Hudson continues. "I don't want to excuse any of my behavior, but I was under a lot of stress. I had this intense Macroeconomics problem set due, which I couldn't do at all. I was swamped at work. We had that fight. Oh, it was so stupid."

I nod and try to look away. When he notices my gaze moving, he takes my chin with his hand and points my head back at him.

"What I'm trying to say, Alice, is that I love you. I'm not confused anymore. I know what I want."

"And what's that?" I ask. I can't believe what he's saying. It sounds like words. Familiar words. They just don't make any sense in that order.

"I want to be with you, silly." He smiles.

"Um," I start to say. I don't even know where to begin.

"Please, Alice." Hudson's eyes plead with mine. "I love you. I know I hurt you again, but I want to make it up to you."

"I don't know," I whisper.

"I know you love me, too," he says, kissing my fingertips. "I just know it. I can feel it now."

Oh, if only it was this simple. Of course I love you, I want to say, but that's not all that matters. There's more to it. There's all this complicated life stuff. All the things that make love so impossible and complex and difficult to handle.

"I love you, too," I say. I don't know what else to say. I want to tell him something true. For a second, I don't want to lie. I don't want to be a fraud. Every moment we've had together has felt like an un-truth ever since we got back from Atlantic City.

"That's great." Hudson's eyes light up, but I shake my head. "What? What's wrong?" he asks.

Tell him. Tell him now. Tell him that you accidentally married his roommate. He'll forgive you. If you tell him now. I open my mouth to say it, but nothing comes out.

"I'm not sure that's enough," I say.

"Of course it is, Alice," Hudson says. He moves over to my side of the table. There's warmth pouring out of him, actual heat, and it wraps me in a warm blanket of love. He puts his arm around my shoulder, lifting up my head. He presses his lips onto mine. I want to push him away. He doesn't know what a horrible person I am and how wrong it is for him to love me. I don't. I can't. I want to stay in this moment forever. I don't know if it will come again.

"Love is all there is, Alice," Hudson says through the kiss. I can feel a wide smile form on his lips. "Don't you know that?"

"No, there are other things. Things that complicate love," I say, pulling away from him. If you knew what I did, you wouldn't think that love is all there is, I say to him silently, in my own head.

"No." He kisses me again, parting my lips with his and running his tongue over mine. "All you need is love. That's all anyone needs."

"That sounds nice," I say with a smile.

"What's wrong, Alice?" Hudson says. His face grows more serious. Concerned.

"Nothing." I shrug. Just tell him. Open your mouth and say, so this is what happened that weekend we went to Atlantic City. We got really drunk, and I mean really drunk, and Dylan and I accidentally got married, but it was just an accident. We're going to get an annulment. Everything's going to be okay. Let's just pretend that everything is the way it was. Like this never happened. I mean, all you need is love, right? You love me and I love you. That's all you have to say. Just start talking.

"Alice?" Hudson asks again.

"I don't know, Hudson," I finally manage to say. "Everything is so complicated now. I don't know if we can just go back to the way things were."

"But why? I want to and I can see that you want to, too," he says with a hopeful look on his beautiful face. I inhale and breathe out slowly. So, what if I did? What if I just moved on with this from this moment forward? Wouldn't that be something? Of course, I can't. I wouldn't. It would be too wrong.

"Okay." I nod my head. "Okay. Let's do it."

"Okay?" Hudson asks. I can see that he can barely believe his ears. "Seriously? You want to get back together?"

Still not into you

"Yes." I nod. "I love you. Very much. More than anything."

"Oh my God, Alice." Hudson wraps himself around me. I can feel him smelling the top of my head as he hugs me. I feel his body shaking next to mine.

"I love you," he whispers as he pulls away.

When I look up at him, I see a few tiny tears building up at the bottom of his eyelids. Hudson isn't much of a crier. I've only seen him cry on two occasions—once when his grandmother died and another when his best friend got into an awful car wreck and we didn't know if he would live or die.

"I'm so, so sorry about everything," he mumbles.

"Me, too," I whisper. "I'm sorry about everything."

22

Hudson is sorry about the past. He wishes it would go away. I'm sorry about the future. I wish that it wouldn't come, or at least, that the truth wouldn't come out. Sitting across from him right now, it almost feels possible. Like I can actually get this marriage annulled without him ever finding out about it. Maybe we can just…pretend that this never happened. Maybe we can just start off where we had left off.

"I'm so happy, Alice," Hudson says, leaning back in his chair. His smile turns into a laugh, which then shakes his whole body. Loose strands of hair fall into his face as he rocks back and forth. He tucks some behind his ears, over and over, but they keep getting untucked.

Our eyes meet and, this time, I don't let go.

"Me, too," I whisper.

"Let's get out of here," he says, taking my hand.

I don't know where we're going. I let Hudson lead the way. I'm okay with wherever he decides to take me. I just want to be with him.

Hudson leans close to me. We're in his room. No one else is home. His fingers run along my jawline and bury themselves in my hair. He gets closer. I feel his breath on my lips, but he doesn't kiss me. I pull forward and try to press my lips onto his, but he stops me. He demands that I wait. He leans down and runs his lips over my neck. His lips are smooth and gentle. Soft.

I bury my hands in his hair. Slowly, I pull his head up to mine. I have to taste him. I want his tongue inside my mouth. When our lips finally meet, shivers run throughout my body. His tongue is strong and rough. Hudson grabs my neck. With each breath, his kisses get more and more passionate. Now, he is kissing me as if he's trying to prove something. I let him. I kiss him back with the same intensity and power. I want to prove something, too. No matter what happens in the future, I want him to remember this moment. This moment in which only we existed and the whole world could stop spinning upon our command.

Slowly, Hudson removes my sweater and I pull off his t-shirt. He unbuckles his pants and steps out of them. He pushes me down onto his bed and

Still not into you

unzips my skinny jeans. He kisses my legs as he rolls them off me. My knees grow weak, as Hudson's kisses intensify. He runs his fingers over my breasts, toeing the line between pleasure and pain.

As my hands make my way up his naked body, they feel rushed and unstable. Urgent. The muscles in his stomach flex and I feel each distinct muscle of his six-pack. I lean back, enjoying the moment, looking forward to what's next.

Hudson undoes my bra and tosses it on the floor. He then grabs my hips and tugs at my panties with his teeth. I wiggle my body to help him along, enjoying the ferociousness of the moment.

Slowly, he eases himself inside of me. I feel myself welcoming him inside. My fingers dig into his shoulders and my hips start to move up and down on their own. I'm getting close. I look up at him. Our eyes meet briefly. I can see that he's getting close, too. A moment later, a warm sensation pulses through my body. My legs get numb and I dig my toes into the bed.

"Oh, Hudson," I whisper.

"Alice," he moans, taking one last thrust and collapsing on top of me.

We lie next to each other for a while. Twilight comes and goes and darkness sets in, but neither of us bothers to get out of bed or turn on the light. It's as if we're both trying to hold on to this moment for as long as possible.

"Thank you," Hudson says, propping up his head with his hand. I turn to face him.

"No, thank you," I say.

Hudson flashes a mischievous smile.

"Well, thank you for this, definitely," he says, giving me a peck on the cheek. "But what I meant is thank you for forgiving me. I know that it's not really your specialty and that I must've hurt you a lot with all of my talk about taking a break."

His words sting a little. I can't lie, but he's right. I'm not one to forgive easily. If I weren't in the wrong, if I hadn't just accidentally married our roommate, I'm not so sure we'd be doing this right now.

"I still don't really understand what happened," I say. "Back then."

"To tell you the truth," Hudson says after a moment of silence, "I'm not so sure either. I think it was all that stress I was under. I just sort of cracked up."

"I see." I nod. That's not much of an explanation, but we've been over this a million times. A million explanations later, I am still not completely clear about what really happened.

"So, how's work going?" I ask. "Still as crazy as ever?"

"Yes," Hudson says. "More so, even, I think, but

Still not into you

I have a little bit of a routine now. So, I don't feel so lost all the time. Like I'm playing catch up."

"Do you like it?" I ask. "Do you think it's something you want to do in the future?"

"I don't know," Hudson says, looking up at the ceiling. I can tell he's really thinking about what I had asked.

"I like the internship. I mean, I really think I'm learning a lot," he finally says. "I definitely want to do something with finance or investment banking in the future, I think. I'm just not sure about this particular job. Like the one that Kathryn has."

Agh, Kathryn. Why did he have to bring her up?

"So, how's Kathryn? Did anything happen between you two?" I ask cautiously. I don't want to seem too jealous or concerned. Just like I'm trying to make normal conversation.

"No." He shakes his head definitively. "I'm sorry again about before."

"What? What do you have to be sorry about?" I ask.

"Well, you know, I wasn't entirely truthful back then. I mean, I knew that she liked me. Of course, I did. She told me. Even before she kissed me at the bar that time. I told her about you. But…I guess I should've been even clearer."

I nod. I feel very guilty. I need to tell him the truth. I know that. I owe him the truth, but now I'm even more scared than I was before. Now, I'm terrified. Even a few hours ago, he was sort of my ex. Now he's back to being my boyfriend. I feel like I have the whole world on my shoulders, and it's getting heavier and heavier by the minute.

"Alice?" Hudson turns to me.

"Yeah?"

"Are you okay? You're sort of spacing out for a bit."

"Yeah, I'm fine," I say, nodding. "It has been kind of a long day."

"Okay." He springs out of bed. "Why don't you relax for a bit while I try to put a dent into that Macroeconomics problem set and try being the operative word, of course."

I smile and nod. I watch him get dressed. He gives me a peck on the cheek and leaves the room.

I AM STILL LYING naked in bed and listening to music when I hear Hudson call my name from the living room. It has only been ten minutes since he left, but I suddenly realize that I'm in Hudson's room and Dylan might be back.

"Alice!" Hudson yells.

"What?" I call back, scrambling to put on my clothes. I manage to throw on my sweater and underwear, but I struggle with the jeans. Why did I have to wear skinny jeans today, of all days?

"Alice!"

"I'm coming!"

I roll my bra into a little wad and hide it in my bag. Why can't he just come in here? Why is he yelling like this?

When I walk into the living room, I see Hudson pacing back and forth.

"Hudson?" I ask.

He stops dead in his tracks. When he turns around, I see an expression on his face that I have never seen before. His eyes are empty, his lips are pursed, and his cheeks are devoid of color. I think that someone has died.

"What's wrong?" I run up to him. "Are you okay? What happened?"

I try to put my arms around him, but he shrugs me off.

"What's this?" he says, waving something in my face. I take it out of his hand. It's a postcard with a picture of a casino from Atlantic City. Oh, wait. Not just some casino. *The* casino!

"I don't know," I say, putting on the most innocent look I can. "What is it?"

"Don't bullshit me, Alice," Hudson says, shaking his head. He hands me the postcard. I flip it around and see it. Those words. They will probably stay with me always.

DEAR MR. DYLAN *and Mrs. Alice Summers Worthington,*
  Congratulations on your recent wedding. It was a pleasure

to share this momentous occasion with you. We hope that you will join us again in the near future. As a thank you, we'd like to extend an invitation to you to stay at our hotel for a reduced price.

THERE IS MORE to it than that. The postcard offered us a 50% discount on all future bookings for the year, but, frankly, I stopped reading carefully after I saw the words *Mrs. Worthington* and *wedding*.

"Alice, what's going on?" Hudson asks, taking the postcard out of my hand.

23

I take a deep breath. This is my chance.
Hudson knows and he doesn't really even know he knows.

"I have something to tell you," I say. "Can you sit down?"

I can tell by the look on his face that he isn't mad yet. Not even angry. Instead, he has this vacant look in his eyes. Like soldiers do in war movies, right after their friends get blown up. Shell-shocked.

Hudson sits down and I tell him everything. I don't even try to sugar coat it. I just tell him the truth. Exactly as it happened. He listens quietly and doesn't interrupt me once.

"I don't understand," he says after I'm done. "You're actually married?"

I hate that word. It makes me sound so old and worldly and stupid at the same time.

I nod. "Yes, technically, but hopefully not for long."

"To *my best friend*, Dylan?"

I didn't know that they were best friends now. That's news to me. I nod.

"To *our roommate*, Dylan?" Hudson asks. I nod again.

"And you two, what, slept together? On top of that?" he asks.

"I don't know," I say after a moment. "I honestly don't know. Maybe."

"Oh my God, Alice! Oh my God! What were you thinking?" He gets up and starts pacing around the room.

I want him to sit down, but I'm afraid to reach out to him. Afraid that he'll push me away and never talk to me again.

"I wasn't," I say. "I was really upset about us. I wanted to let out some steam. So, we all drank a little too much and I got really drunk."

"Yeah, everyone drank too much, but it was only you and Dylan who got married and slept together. Why? Why did you do that?"

Hudson's eyes search my face. I see longing and desperation in them. I want to make it all go away, but I can't.

"You know what else, you were never going to tell me about this, were you, Alice?" he asks. "If I didn't see this stupid postcard, you and Dylan were

Still not into you

just never going to tell me. You were just going to go on and pretend like nothing had happened."

"No…we weren't," I lie.

"Yes, you were!" he yells in my face. The hair on the back of my arms stands up.

"What about Juliet? Does she know?"

I don't reply. I simply look away from him.

"Oh, shit! Juliet knows, doesn't she? She knows?" Hudson says and goes back to pacing. "So, what do you all do? Do you all joke and laugh about this behind my back when I'm not here? Is that what you do?"

"No, no," I say. Before I can get a hold of myself, I run up to him and throw my arms around his shoulders. "No, I'm so, so sorry, Hudson. You have to believe me."

"Get the fuck off me!" He pushes me away. Hard. I lose my balance and fall to the floor. "I can't believe you, Alice," Hudson says, shaking his head. "I poured my heart out to you. I apologized for just flirting with Kathryn and you just went out there and married our roommate. My best friend. What the fuck, Alice? Who the hell are you?"

I don't know. I don't know who I am. All I know is that I'm not the person that I once was and I'm not sure if I'll ever be her again.

"Are you okay, Alice? What are you doing on the floor?" Dylan walks into the living room.

"You!" Hudson yells. I don't see him run past

me, but suddenly he and Dylan are intertwined and withering around on the floor.

"Hudson, stop. Please," I yell, but it's to no avail. He punches Dylan in the face. He tries to punch him again, but Dylan blocks the second punch and instead, knees him in the groin.

"Hudson, Dylan, please stop!" I yell at the top of my lungs, but no one is listening to me. They're back at it again. Pushing. Tussling. Fighting. At one moment, Dylan's on top. At the next, Hudson is. Then Dylan again. Back to Hudson. Finally, I manage to grab someone's shoulders. I pull as hard as I can, but he hardly budges.

BAM!

Everything turns to black. I can't see anything. My whole face is tingling and throbbing. When I grab my nose to try to numb the pain, I feel something hot and sticky. I pull my hand away and see that I'm covered in blood. My nose is bleeding. I can't see out of one eye.

"Hudson, what the fuck are you doing?" I hear someone say somewhere very far away. I recognize the voice. It belongs to Dylan, but he's speaking in slow motion.

"Are…you….okay?" Dylan asks me. I see him above me. He's still talking incredibly slowly. I try to say yes, but nothing comes out. My blood over my body is freaking me out. My heart starts to beat faster. My breaths get shallower. My hands and legs go numb. Everything turns blurry.

Still not into you

"Alice? Alice?" I hear someone's voice somewhere above me. It's a female voice. I try to open my eyes, but I only manage to get one open. The light from the lamp causes me great pain and I shut it quickly. The other one doesn't open at all.

"Oh my God, Alice." I hear the girl say again. "What the fuck is wrong with you two?"

"It was an accident. He didn't mean to elbow her," a guy says.

"I don't care. You shouldn't have been fighting in the first place," she says. Juliet. It's Juliet, I decide.

"He started it," the guy says. Suddenly, everything starts to come back to me.

Hudson finding the postcard. Telling him about the accidental wedding. Dylan walking in. Hudson and Dylan fighting. Trying to stop them. Getting elbowed in the face. My nose bleeding. I don't remember this, but that's probably when I must've passed out.

I sit up and look around. I can barely see out of my left eye. The eyelid feels incredibly heavy and I don't have enough strength to lift it. All I can make is a little slit.

"You need to put some ice on that," Juliet says. She goes to the refrigerator and gets me a bag of frozen berries.

"Here. We don't have any peas, but this should do."

"Where's Hudson?" I ask, taking the berries. I press the bag onto my eye. It relieves some of the pain from the swelling but brings about more of a different kind of pain from pressing something so cold onto such a sensitive surface.

"I don't know," she says with a shrug.

"He's outside," Dylan says.

"What the hell happened, Dylan?" I ask.

"I don't know, what the hell happened to you? You weren't supposed to tell him anything! Don't you remember that little promise?"

"I wasn't going to, but that stupid hotel sent us a postcard thanking us for getting married there, with some sort of discount for future stays. He saw it," I say.

I point to the dining room table where the postcard, which has ruined my life, lies innocently.

"Shit," Dylan says, picking it up. "Why would they do this?"

No one says anything for a few moments.

"It's probably for the best," I finally say. "He was going to find out anyway."

"Not like this," Dylan says.

Dylan goes to his room and then comes out with a concerned look on his face.

"Do you know where my phone is?" he asks. "I just had it."

"I saw it earlier," Juliet says. "It was on the floor when you two were fighting."

Juliet helps Dylan look for his phone while I continue to sit motionlessly in a daze.

"It's not here," Dylan says. His voice is getting

Still not into you

frantic. What's the big deal? I wonder. Who the hell cares about a phone right now?

"It's not here, Alice," he says.

"So?"

"So? So? Don't you know what this means?"

"What?"

"Hudson must've taken it," Dylan says. His face drains of all color. I stare at him.

"Why would he want your phone? He has his own."

"Because his has Peyton's number on it," Juliet says quietly.

Oh, no, I think. I shake my head.

"Hudson wouldn't do that," I say slowly.

"Of course he would," Dylan says. "He's really pissed at us."

"Do you know her number?" Juliet asks. "You can use my phone."

Dylan walks around, trying to remember. No, he shakes his head.

"I used to know her old one, but she recently got a new one with a New Haven number," he says.

"Wait, I called her a few weekends back. I think I can find it. What's the area code?"

"203," Dylan says.

Juliet scrolls through her phone. Eventually she finds it and hands Dylan her phone. He's about to dial it, but then hesitates.

"I can't," he says, shaking his head.

"You have to know," Juliet says.

"How will I know? Do I just ask her?" he asks.

"You won't have to," Juliet says. "If he called her and told her...you'll know right when she answers."

Dylan breathes in deeply. I look at Juliet. We both seem to hold our breath.

"Peyton?" Dylan says after she finally picks up. "Hey."

His face simply grows white. All blood drains from his cheeks and his lips turn almost blue. Dylan's shoulders slouch and he drops down to the couch as if his legs can't hold him up anymore. Without saying a word, he looks down at the phone.

"She hung up," he says, even though no explanations are needed. Juliet and I both know that Peyton knows.

A WEEK PASSES. My eye manages to heal somewhat, not look so black and blue. I can see out of it again. Unfortunately, my life is a little harder to heal. Hudson doesn't return any of my calls or texts and he refuses to talk to me. One day we ride the elevator down together. No matter how hard I try, he ignores me. I'm not even a stranger to him anymore. I'm worse. I'm a ghost. He doesn't even acknowledge my existence.

The worst part? I know that I deserve it. I should've just told him the truth right away. I

Still not into you

shouldn't have led him on and acted like everything was fine when he made up with me. I shouldn't have done a million things, but if I were to do it again, I would. I wanted to kiss him. I wanted to be with him. If only one last time. Looking back now, I wonder if I knew that it was going to be our last time together. Maybe that's why I went along with it. Seized the day, so to speak.

I made an unusual discovery this week. I didn't know how difficult it was to explain why I had a black eye and make someone believe that it was an accident. For some reason, I came up with a ridiculous story—that I fell into a corner of a bookshelf. It seemed so reasonable, but when I ran it by a few people who asked me with a concerned look on their face what had happened, I could tell right away that, though they nodded and said they were sorry, none of them believed me. Luckily, my eye started to heal and fewer and fewer people asked me about it as time passed.

Outside of my roommates, the only people who know the truth about what had happened are Tea and Dr. Greyson. They were the only ones with whom I actually talked about all this in detail and told the truth. When I talked to Tea about it, she acted like a good friend. She didn't make judgements and she didn't give me advice. I messed up so much that I'm beyond advice. I don't want to hear it. I can't take any of it in. I just want to run away screaming whenever someone (like Juliet) offers it up. Dr. Greyson, on the other hand, isn't much of an advice giver. When I talked to her, I got the impression that she actually thinks that I secretly want my whole life to fall apart. Like I'm on some sort of mission to destroy my life and I'm not. Not really. At least I hope not.

Honestly, talking about it doesn't help much. Instead, it makes me feel like I'm dwelling on something that I can never get over or change and that makes me feel like crap. So recently, I've come to a decision. I'm not going to talk about it anymore. I'm not even going to think about it. If Hudson doesn't want to talk about it, then why should I? What's done is done. It's over. It was a terrible mistake. All I can do now is try to move on. If only the legal system understood the urgency with which I wanted to move on…

24

The legal system moves at its own pace and it cannot be rushed no matter how hard you try. Dealing with it is an exercise in patience. What I find out from Dylan and later confirm on my own by researching the topic online is that an annulment is incredibly difficult to get in the state of New York.

I've heard the word "annulment" many times before, but I didn't actually know what it meant. Apparently, an annulment is a finding by a court that a marriage is invalid or void and this finding allows the court to make it as if the marriage never occurred. This is what both Dylan and I want, but it doesn't look like it's something that can happen.

"I can't believe that we can't get an annulment," I say. Dylan is sitting on the couch texting someone.

"We've been over this already," he says without looking up.

"I know," I sigh. "But what if…"

"Look, here, let me read it to you," he says, cutting me off.

He already told me this and I read a lot about it already online, but I still feel like there must be a way. Dylan searches for something on his phone and clears his throat.

"There are various grounds that allow either spouse to bring the action to annul the marriage," Dylan reads. "These are the grounds. Either spouse had not reached the age of legal consent, eighteen years of age. That doesn't apply to us."

I nod.

"Either spouse is incurably incapable of having sexual intercourse. Either spouse has incurable insanity for at least five years after marriage. Either spouse could not give actual consent to the marriage (could not understand the effect, nature, and the consequences of marriage)."

"Oh, that's us!" I say. "We were drunk. We didn't actually understand the effect and consequences of marriage."

"You didn't let me finish," Dylan says. "Either spouse could not give actual consent to the marriage, could not understand the nature, effect, and consequences of marriage, *as a result of* some mental incapacity or deficiency."

"We were drunk," I say.

"That's not a mental incapacity," he says.

"Are you serious? We got married and didn't

remember. If that's not a mental incapacity or deficiency, I don't know what is."

"Maybe," he says. "But that's not what it means legally."

Dylan turns back to his phone and continues to read.

"Either spouse consented to the marriage as a result of force or duress of the other."

"Again, I was drunk, I consented as a result of duress," I say.

"*Again*, this doesn't apply," Dylan says. "Force in legal terms is a really high standard. It's as if I held a gun to your head to get you to marry me."

"Finally, either spouse's consent was obtained by fraud," Dylan reads. "The fraud must go to the essence of the marriage contract, and then only the injured spouse can obtain the annulment."

"So, none of these will work?" I ask. He shakes his head.

"So, what do we do now?"

"We have to get a divorce," Dylan says.

"What does that entail?" I ask. Dylan shrugs.

"I have no idea, but I'll ask our family attorney."

So, this is certain now. An annulment is not an option. We can't just make this marriage go away and pretend that it never happened. We have to get a divorce. A divorce. Divorce. That word is so strange, I can barely comprehend its meaning. After we get a divorce, will I be a divorcee? Some sad, middle-aged woman who's bitter about men? No, of course not. I'll still be a nineteen-year-old girl who made a terrible mistake. It still doesn't sound pleasant.

Dylan and I don't say a word to each other for a while. He hasn't talked about it with me yet, but I heard from Juliet that Peyton refuses to talk to him. He hasn't seen her since Hudson told her, even though he went to her dorm on two separate occasions to try to explain. She flat out refuses to see him. Hudson and Dylan? They're still roommates, but they're also ships passing in the night. Hudson is barely home and when he is, he's usually asleep. I'm not sure they've spoken since the fight either.

"We really fucked up, didn't we?" I ask when I turn to Dylan and see that we were thinking about the same thing.

"Big time," he says quietly.

"Do you think they'll ever forgive us?" I ask.

"I don't know," he whispers. The thought of that sends shivers up my spine.

THE PARTY for that Friday night had been planned a long time ago and we can't cancel it now. It was Dylan's idea, but we have all invited people and asked them to bring people, so there's no way to let everyone know it's off. The only thing is to go through with it and host it. Dylan gets the alcohol and the cups and Juliet and I get the food and the

Still not into you

decorations. Juliet actually seems excited and gets a little carried away in the party favors section.

"Are you sure we need so many?" I ask.

"Yes," she says, throwing more into the cart. "I've been living in the middle of a war zone for a couple of weeks now and I need to let loose. At first, it was fiery and exciting, so that was fun. For me. Now, the whole place has become some sort of Cold War zone. No one talks to anyone anymore. It's boring and tense. This party is exactly what we need to move on with our lives."

"Move on?" I ask.

"Listen, you and Dylan act like you're the only people in the world getting a divorce, but you're not. Lots of people do it and they don't mope around like you two. So, you made a mistake? So what? Nothing too terrible has happened. It's not like you killed someone."

"You definitely have a way of putting everything in perspective," I say sarcastically. "I mean, I guess I should be glad that instead of just ruining my life, I didn't actually kill someone."

The sarcasm is lost on her. She either doesn't get it or chooses to actively ignore it. Instead, she goes to the next aisle over and drops a few more decorative banners into the cart.

25

Later that night, our dorm is flooded with people. Everyone is standing around, drinking, laughing, and having a good time. Two separate beer pong games form and Dylan is only too happy to organize and oversee both. He's a beer pong king and is quite a stickler for rules and regulations. While he is taking advantage of the party as an excuse to get plastered, I decide to not drink at all tonight. Nothing good has come from my drinking this semester and I need a break. I pour myself another cup of soda into a red plastic cup and try to join a conversation about the Oscars. Who is nominated? Who isn't? Who should've been? I can't follow what anyone is saying. I know what they're saying, but none of the words are making sense in sentence form. My mind is wandering. I can't focus on anything.

"Don't you think so, Alice?" the girl next to me

asks. I have no idea what she's talking about. She lives down the hall from me. I've seen her a million times before. We've exchanged pleasantries in the elevator. I know that she's majoring in dance, but I can't even remember her name.

"Yeah," I say with a nod. Everyone waits for me to continue, but I can't. "Listen, does anyone want anything to eat or another drink?"

Everyone shakes their heads and goes back to what they were doing. I head toward the dining room table and top off my drink with more soda. I want to look busy and like I'm having fun. I pace around the room saying hi to people, but not staying long enough to engage in actual conversation. My mind wanders, but it keeps coming back to one thing—Hudson. Will he come? I search the room and all the new faces that have shown up in the last half hour. Hudson's not one of them. Maybe he won't come. I wouldn't be surprised. Even though it is Dylan and I who have done this horrible thing, it is he who has been paying for it. It is he who has been staying away. We didn't ask him to leave. I didn't want him to stay away, bt he has ostracized himself.

Then, just as I'm about to give up hope, I see him.

He walks through the front door in his suit, tie, and polished shoes. He is dressed like an adult, like someone with a real job. The girls at the party are dressed nicely, taking the opportunity to wear nice

Still not into you

outfits for once in college, but the guys are a total disaster. In comparison to them, he looks like a god.

Unlike many guys our age who look like they don't belong in a suit and like they are playing at being adults by putting on their dad's, Hudson embodies his. He doesn't look oppressed by the stiff collar or the perfectly creased pants. He doesn't look like the tie is one step from strangling him or the cuffs are cutting off his circulation and his willingness to live. No, his body belongs in the suit. He looks like he could sleep and eat and run in it. Like the two were meant to be together.

He walks toward the dining room table and pours a drink. The red cup looks out of place. He should be holding a perfectly polished glass with scotch or maybe a martini. I wait for him to take a sip—to see his elegance at work. Instead, he turns around and hands it to someone behind him.

Her.

Kathryn.

The woman in red.

Oh. My. God.

I want to scream. Tear my eyes out. Tear her eyes out. Pound my fists on the table.

I continue to stand here motionless. Expressionless. Taking little shallow breaths that are barely enough to keep my body from shutting down.

Kathryn smiles graciously and nods. She's about to take her drink from Hudson, but then mimics to him to hold on to it for a second while she removes her coat. Under her coat, she's wearing a little black dress. It's tight around all the right places, accentuating her beautiful figure. I watch as Hudson looks her up and down while taking her coat. Her collarbones are adorned with a delicate necklace with blue gemstones that bring out her eyes. Her lips are lined with a luscious red lipstick.

Agh! I look away from them. I think I'm going to scream otherwise.

"Hudson's here," Juliet says under her breath. She nudges me in his direction.

"I know," I say and try to walk away, but she follows me.

"Where are you going?"

"I have to leave," I say.

"Why?"

"Did you see his date?" I ask. Juliet looks around.

"Oh, yeah! That's the same girl from the bar, huh?"

I roll my eyes. Juliet can be very dense sometimes. Bullheaded. I'm not sure if it's on purpose.

"Alice." I hear someone call my name. I pretend that I didn't hear it, but he's persistent.

"Alice?" he says, grabbing my arm. I know who it is. I take a deep breath before turning around.

"I'd like to introduce you to someone," Hudson says. His eyes sparkle. He wants to make me suffer. I deserve this.

Still not into you

"This is Kathryn," he says. "Kathryn, this is my ex-girlfriend, Alice."

"Nice to meet you." I extend my hand. Her hand is warm and inviting, while mine is ice cold. I feel like it's getting sweaty as we touch and pull away as quickly as I can.

"Nice to meet you, too," she says in a kind, soothing voice. There's a tinge of malice in it and it makes me hate her even more. She isn't proud or trying to rub it in my face. Why can't she be like every other girl? Why does she have to be…genuine?

"I've heard a lot about you," Kathryn says.

"Well, don't believe everything you hear," I say jokingly. I mean it like a casual joke, but it comes out all wrong. Bitter, somehow.

"Oh, no, not all. Hudson had nothing but good things to say," she says with a smile. I can tell that my comment made her do a double take.

"Well, now I know that you're lying," I say with a smile.

Kathryn takes a deep breath and a sip of her drink. I can tell that this moment is as uncomfortable for her as it is for me. We both blame Hudson for it, but Hudson isn't sorry. He wants to pick a fight.

26

"So," he says with a cocky attitude. He looks around the room.

"What?" I ask when he doesn't continue.

"Where's your husband?" he asks. Now I get it. He was just waiting for the right moment to deliver his blow. I didn't know he was such a good actor. He has got excellent timing.

"Hudson," Kathryn says. She puts her hand on his arm to try to get him to calm down. That used to be my job. I've been laid off. "Hudson, calm down," she says under her breath. I try to hold back the smile that's forming on my lips. What she doesn't know is that he's perfectly calm. Decisive. This is exactly what he wants to do.

"What? We're all friends here, right? Alice? I'm just making small talk. Just wondering where your dear hubby is," he says sarcastically.

Okay, I'll play along. I look around the room.

"Dylan's right over there," I say, pointing to the beer pong table. "Do you want to talk to him?"

"Yes," he says reluctantly, taking a beat. I've called him on his bluff. "I'd like that," Hudson adds.

I call Dylan over. When he sees the three of us, the expression on his face changes from exuberant and laid back to reserved in a moment. He stares at me. I shrug to apologize. There's nothing I can do.

"Dylan, I'd like you to meet my…friend," Hudson says, searching for the right word for who Kathryn is to him. The way he says it, we both know that it's not true.

"This is Kathryn," he says. "Kathryn, this is Dylan Worthington. My roommate and Alice's husband."

"Not for long," Dylan says. "It's very nice to meet you."

I look at Kathryn. As they shake hands, Kathryn is so embarrassed, she looks like she wants the floor to open and swallow her right there and then. Hudson remains oblivious, either completely unaware of how uncomfortable she and everyone else is, or callous to it. At first, I gave him the benefit of the doubt, but now, I'm not so sure. He's beaming with pride. The wrong kind. He wants us to suffer and he doesn't care if Kathryn suffers along with us.

"Not for long?" Hudson asks. "Is the honeymoon over already?"

"There never was one, Hudson. You know

that," Dylan says. Then he turns to Kathryn to explain. "It was an accident. We're getting it taken care of."

"I see," she mumbles.

"An accident? Oh, is that what you're calling this?" Hudson says, taking a step back insulted. "People accidentally rear-end a car. They accidentally forget their keys and get locked out of their house. People do NOT accidentally marry their best friend's girlfriend!"

"Okay, Hudson, calm down," Kathryn says, sternly this time.

"I am calm," he says, shrugging her hand off his shoulder. "But seriously. Why don't we take a poll? I mean, let's ask all of these people at the party whether what you two did can be considered an accident."

None of us say anything. I feel like I'm watching a runaway train and I can't do anything to make it stop.

"Hey, everyone! Everyone! Can I have your attention please?" Hudson says loudly. After a few moments, everyone quiets down and turns their attention to him.

"My roommate here, my best friend, Dylan Worthington, went to Atlantic City a few weeks ago with my other roommate and my girlfriend. The girl who was the love of my life, or so I'd thought. They got married and slept together. They are saying that it was an accident. Now, my question to you all is, can we actually call it an accident? I mean, to me an accident is running into something or calling the wrong number. Not marrying your best friend's girl."

We all wait for someone to say something. Each second that passes feels like an eternity. Then a smart-ass from the back yells out, "It depends on how much they had to drink!"

Everyone laughs.

"See, that's what they keep telling me," Hudson says. "But the thing is that all of you in this room have been drunk plenty and how many of you can say that you got married while you were drunk?"

"Maybe she just got tired of your moaning, man. Maybe your roommate doesn't complain so much," the guy in the back says again.

Everyone laughs with him and turns back to doing what they were doing. Hudson shakes his head and drops his shoulders. He's embarrassed. I'm sorry for him, but I can't help but give out a sigh of relief.

"I'm sorry, Hudson," Dylan says. "I'm really sorry."

"I don't care," he says, shaking his head. Hudson turns away from him, so Dylan turns to Kathryn.

"We're getting a divorce. As soon as possible. We just have to get a lawyer and this will be over. Soon."

"I know," Kathryn says.

She's speaking for Hudson. I hate how I seemed

Still not into you

to have been replaced in a second, but I can't blame anyone but myself and the alcohol.

"Well, I'm sorry it didn't work out," Hudson says. "I was really rooting for you two."

The sarcasm in his voice is filled with pain. I wish there was something I could do to help him. To make all of this go away, but I'm helpless.

"You're a real asshole, Hudson," Dylan says.

"Oh, I'm an asshole? Seriously, man? I'm the asshole?" Hudson asks. He's at a loss for words. I don't know why Dylan had to say that. He was on the right track with his apologies. Now… everything's even worse.

"I'm sorry." Dylan turns to me, as if to answer what I was thinking. "I've apologized for this plenty. I am sorry. I'm not making excuses, but if he doesn't want to accept my apology, there's nothing I can do."

"Fuck you, Dylan!" Hudson says.

"No, fuck you," Dylan says.

We're a second away from yet another fight and I don't know how to stop it. Luckily, Kathryn does.

"I'm leaving," she says, grabbing her coat away from Hudson. He's caught off guard.

"What?" he asks.

"I'm leaving," she says again. She puts on her coat and puts her cup on the table.

"It was nice to meet you," she says to me and heads toward the door.

"Where are you going?" Hudson yells after her.

"I'm leaving," Kathryn says without turning around.

"Why?" Hudson asks, running up to her.

"Because you're acting like a child. I didn't come here with you for you to act like that."

They continue to argue, but everything else they say is out of earshot. All I know is that Hudson isn't able to get her to stay and they take their arguing outside.

The night proceeds at a more even pace after that. Dylan and I avoid each other. I spot Tea and Tanner and try to lose myself in a conversation with them. They were present for the scene that Hudson caused, but once he leaves, they thankfully don't ask me anything more about him. Juliet hooks up with a guy I've never seen before, but luckily does not invite him to spend the night.

When I go to bed that night after cleaning up after the party, I'm well aware of the fact that Hudson isn't back yet. I try not to think about it and what it means. He's with Kathryn and they're probably at her place. Instead, I just bury my head under the covers and force myself to fall asleep.

27

The following morning, I sleep in late. The party raged on until after 3 a.m. and I don't get up until well after ten. My head is pounding. I wrap myself up in my robe and drag my feet into the kitchen to get a cup of coffee. My thinking is all blurry and the light streaming through the windows is too bright. I pull the shades down. Plop. They make a loud noise, startling someone sleeping on the couch.

"What the hell?" he asks. I turn around. It's Dylan. "Why are you making so much noise?" he asks with his eyes still closed.

"Why are you sleeping out here?" I ask, ignoring his question.

He doesn't respond. I look at the door, and there, on the handle, I see a Do Not Disturb sign. Not just any sign. I'm well familiar with that one. That's the Do Not Disturb sign that Hudson stole from the hotel room in Mammoth, California, where we spent the weekend skiing and making love. That's our Do Not Disturb sign.

Suddenly, the door opens and Kathryn comes out. She's wearing the dress she wore last night and holding her heels in her right hand. Her hair is disheveled and out of control. She's wearing barely any makeup and the eyeliner that she has on looks like it was applied last night, but she still looks as beautiful as ever.

"Hey," she says quietly.

"Hey," I say, taking a deep breath.

I wait for her to run off and leave, but she doesn't. She simply stands in the middle of the room waiting for something, but for what? She keeps eyeing the coffee pot. Then it occurs to me.

"Would you like some coffee?" I ask reluctantly.

"Oh, yes, please!" she says. A huge smile forms on her face. "I simply can't function without it. I don't think I would even be able to find my way home."

I nod and pour her a cup of coffee.

"Hey, listen, I'm so sorry about last night." Kathryn walks up to me. She puts her hand on my arm. Shivers run up my spine. I want to shrug her off, but I don't want to be rude.

"What do you mean?" I manage to utter.

"You know, about Hudson making that whole scene. If I knew that he was planning on doing that…I would've never agreed to come."

Still not into you

"Oh, that, yes. I understand," I say with a nod.

"Can you two please take your chatter somewhere else? My head is killing me," Dylan moans from the couch. He doesn't bother to lift his head off the pillow and his words are muffled and barely comprehensible.

I'm about to reply, but then there's a knock on the door.

Bam. Bam. Bam.

Loud knocks, each one less patient than the last.

"Who could that be?" I ask rhetorically. I open the door. A man in an expensive suit and coat storms past me.

"Dylan! Dylan Worthington!" he yells at the top of his lungs.

Dylan opens his eyes and jumps back into the couch. There's sheer terror in his eyes. I look at the man before him. He's fuming. It looks like smoke is about to come out of his ears, but his suit and tie and coat remain perfectly coiffed and put together. His newly shined shoes shine in the sunlight even though the streets are full of slush and sleet.

"What the hell are you thinking, Dylan?" the man yells, reaching for something in his front pocket.

"Dad—" Dylan says.

Ah, that's who it is. Kathryn and I exchange looks.

"What is this?" Mr. Worthington waves a large piece of paper in Dylan's face.

"What is it?" Dylan asks.

"This, my darling son," Mr. Worthington says quietly, his voice saturated with sarcasm, "this is a bill from Tiffany's."

"Oh," Dylan mumbles under his breath.

"So, imagine my surprise," Mr. Worthington turns to Kathryn and me. I get the sense that this man is used to speaking to large groups of people and he relishes the sound of his voice, "when I walk into Tiffany's this morning to buy a diamond ring for my future fiancée and discover that my son, Mr. Worthington, already has an account with them."

"Shit," Dylan says.

"Yes, that's right. 'Is something wrong with the other ring you purchased? Or would you like to exchange it?' the nice woman at the counter asks me. I, of course, have no idea what she's talking about. I haven't been to Tiffany's in years, not since Dylan's mom and I divorced. So, I have no idea what she's talking about. So, I ask her to educate me."

"I'm sorry," Dylan whispers.

"You know what I find out?" Mr. Worthington asks. He's speaking to everyone in the room, but he's focused on me. "Do you?" he asks when I don't respond.

"No," I say, shaking my head.

"What I find out is that apparently I already bought a two-carat diamond ring from them.

Still not into you

Apparently, I had spent $40,000 there two weeks ago!"

"I can explain," Dylan says with a whimper, but his dad doesn't let him.

"A $40,000 ring? Are you insane, Dylan? An engagement ring should be two months of your salary. The last thing I remember is that your salary last year was zero. A big fat zero. So, what does that mean, Dylan? That means that the only ring that you could've gotten your Peyton is a ring pop because that's all you can afford."

"Not Peyton," Juliet says. I don't know how long she's been standing there, but she's never one to avoid drama.

"Excuse me?" Mr. Worthington asks.

"Dylan didn't marry Peyton," Juliet says, shaking her head. "He married Alice."

"What?" Mr. Worthington yells. His face gets flushed and the pupils of his eyes dilate so much it looks like his eyes fill with blackness.

"Wait a second," Dylan says. "Why did you go to Tiffany's?"

What the hell is Dylan talking about? His dad is about to murder us all and he's questioning him? I start to inch my way to the back of the room. If Mr. Worthington explodes, I want to be as far away from him as possible.

"I'm going to ask Cynthia to marry me," Mr. Worthington announces.

"What?" Dylan asks.

Just at that moment, the door to his room opens and Hudson comes out. Perfect timing, as usual.

"Cynthia? You're going to ask Cynthia to marry you? Are you insane?" Dylan asks. He's no longer a scared little boy afraid to make his father mad. He's now standing right in front of his dad, challenging him. He's indignant and his mouth is full of anger and venom.

"Yes, Cynthia." Mr. Worthington shrugs. He looks as surprised by Dylan's temperament as we all are.

"Cynthia is four years older than I am." Dylan turns to me and explains. "She's twenty-three years old. My dad apparently doesn't think that there's anything inappropriate about that."

"Age is just a number," Mr. Worthington says.

"Yeah, right," Dylan says.

"Hey, why are you questioning me anyway? I wasn't the one who secretly got married to a stranger and got her a…" Mr. Worthington looks down at the piece of paper in his hand. Out of the corner of my eye, I can see that a picture of my ring is at the top. "The two carat Tiffany Embrace diamond ring," he reads from the printout. "It's bead-set diamonds exquisitely accentuate a round brilliant center stone in a setting that evokes glamour and romance. All for a price of $44,100! You two were engaged for how long? An hour?"

"You got her a 44 *thousand* dollar ring?" Juliet

Still not into you

whispers. Her eyes light up and I think she's going to faint.

Honestly, the ring looked nice, but I had no idea it was so much money.

"You know what the best thing is? He put it on his father's credit card. How perfect is that?" Mr. Worthington says sarcastically.

"He got you an engagement ring?" Hudson asks quietly. His voice is barely audible, but everyone turns to look at him.

"I'm not going to keep it," I say. It's the only thing I can say.

"You got her an engagement ring?" he asks Dylan.

"So what?" Dylan asks. He's taken aback, I can tell, but I get the feeling that he's not apologizing as long as his dad's here.

"So what?" Mr. Worthington yells. "I was going to get my actual fiancée a $30,000 ring, but my son went out and splurged on forty-four grand of my money on some stranger!"

"She's not a stranger," Dylan says. "Alice, this is my dad, Mr. Worthington. Dad, this is Alice Summers. My roommate and wife."

"Oh, please." Mr. Worthington rolls his eyes.

"What? You think this marriage is a joke? Well, it's not," Dylan says with a shrug.

"What the hell are you talking about?" I whisper.

"Look, Dylan, even your wife knows it's a joke." Mr. Worthington laughs.

"Well, it's not. I wanted to marry her and I did. There's nothing you can do about it."

I shake my head. No, no, no. What is he talking about? Suddenly, my whole body starts to shake uncontrollably. I turn to Hudson. He can't actually believe this. Why is Dylan doing this? Hudson just grabs his jacket and walks out. I follow him. I can't stay in that room any longer.

"Hudson! Hudson!" I run after him, catching him by the elevator. "Please, wait," I say. The button pointing down is lit up and I know we don't have much time.

"He gave you a ring?" he asks. There is sadness on his face and disappointment. It looks like he's going to cry at any moment. He takes a deep breath, trying to hold back tears.

"He got me a ring, but I've already given it back to him. We're getting a divorce. This all has been a terrible mistake," I say. I'm speaking fast, a little fast, but I want to be able to get everything out before the elevator comes.

"He got you a ring, Alice," Hudson says with a shrug. As if that means something. As if it signifies something important. "And a really expensive ring," he adds.

"So what? That's Dylan. If he gets something, then he goes all out, but it doesn't mean a thing. I don't care about that ring."

Still not into you

"It's a two-carat ring, Alice. It cost almost fifty thousand dollars."

"It was just a splurge. A mistake from a night full of mistakes," I say. "Why does it matter what kind of ring it is?"

The elevator doors open.

"I don't know," Hudson says, stepping inside, "but it does."

The elevator doors close and he disappears, leaving me alone. I've never felt so alone before. This is over. Really over. My legs crumple underneath me. I drop to the floor. Tears rush down my face. I can't stop them even if I want to. I just let them wash over me. Maybe they can wash away my mistakes. Probably not.

28

Day turns into night and into day again. I lose track of time. I cry for so long that my eyes feel like someone's slicing them with razor blades and my chest starts to physically hurt from the pain. Eventually, the tears dry up. There are no more. The pain remains, but it's as if it's happening to someone else. I'm detached from it. Separated, somehow. Now, there's just a dark cloud that descends around me. One that I can't shake no matter what I do.

The next two weeks are consumed by melancholy. Hours blend into days and days into nights. I become something of a zombie. I don't cry much anymore; I just wander around lost. Detached from the world. Unreachable. I avoid everyone. I stay on campus for as long as I can, wandering the busy stacks of the library. When I do come home, I avoid everyone except Juliet, whom I can't really avoid, even if I try. Luckily, she has the good sense to pretty much leave me to my own devices. She doesn't pester me with questions and she doesn't ask me how I'm feeling. Mainly, she just leaves me be, which is exactly what I want. As for Hudson and Dylan, I don't see them at all. I can't. I don't think I'd have the strength to deal with my feelings if I were to see Hudson again and I'm too mad at Dylan. I can't believe that he went out of his way to say those things to his father—those things that hurt me to the bottom of my core. He doesn't want to be married to me. He doesn't want to be engaged to me. I, of all people, know how much he has regretted marrying me instead of Peyton. At least with Peyton, there's a history. They love each other and they have for a long time. Even if they were to marry by accident and then get divorced…well, that seems just like something out of their story.

So, if that's true, why did he have to go and tell everyone that he wanted to marry me? Why did he have to get such a big ring? Why did he have to throw it in his father's face? There are some things that I will probably never understand, but I will talk about it with him, one of these days. Just not now. Not yet.

Despite all of my melancholy and lonesomeness, I did manage to come to a decision. A pretty important one, too. I'm going to transfer to University of Southern California next year. It's something that I had been thinking about ever since

Still not into you

this whole mess with Hudson happened. Now I think that getting out of town and going to a completely different school will be the answer to my problems. I know it looks like I'm running away. It sort of feels like that, too, but I honestly don't think I can solve my problems by staying here. They are too complicated and convoluted. No amount of talking will make Hudson understand what happened or forgive me for what I've done. No amount of talking will allow me to forgive him for sleeping with Kathryn or for starting this whole thing in the first place. At this point, it feels like all we can hope for is space. Distance. Space, distance, and time will allow both of us to move on and, perhaps one day, be in that nice space again where we can talk to each other without wanting to kill each other.

USC will be my opportunity to start over. It's a good school in a warm climate near my home. I know LA. LA is my home. Nothing bad, nothing this bad, has ever happened to me there. It sounds like the best thing. I'm only in my freshman year and I can barely see myself making it through this winter intact.

It is with this attitude of cautious optimism and hopefulness that I walk into my Public Speaking class that Friday and raise my hand to make my first real speech. I have not had anything to drink, and I'm under no mind-altering substances, not even caffeine. Surprisingly, the jitters and the fear that plagued my other speeches didn't accompany this one. No, it's like I'm a completely different person now. I clear my throat and look down at my notecards. The assignment is to give a public speech in a professional situation and I've prepared a lecture on Jane Austen. I did my midterm paper on Jane Austen for my Victorian Literature class and I give a cautious, but thorough, speech on her life and work. Yes, I rely on the notecards a little too much. Yes, I avoid eye contact with almost all students in the class and instead choose to look out into space, somewhere beyond their sight lines. Overall? Overall, the speech goes incredibly well. I speak clearly and my voice only shakes a little bit when I forget to breathe. I take a few sips of water as my mouth runs dry, but I don't rush through them and I don't worry about tipping over the water bottle and everyone laughing at me.

"I don't know what it is, but something about me feels different now," I tell Dr. Greyson at our next meeting. I'm going on and on about the success of my speech and how in awe I am over the whole experience.

"What do you think it is?" she asks, taking off her reading glasses and letting them dangle around her neck on the ornate leather rope.

"I'm not sure." I shrug and really think about it. "I sort of think it has something to do with everything that has happened. In the beginning of the semester, I was so focused on Hudson and our relationship and how he wasn't helping me prepare for the speeches that I was paralyzed by them. Now—now that everything happened as it happened—I don't know, it feels like I've been through too much to almost care what those people think."

"Very good," Dr. Greyson says, nodding approvingly. "I'm very proud of you for making so much progress, Alice."

"What progress did I make?" I ask.

"You're giving yourself a voice. When you first came here, you were lost in your own mind. You didn't care what you thought and felt. You only seemed to care about what other people thought and felt about you. It's almost like you, the inside you, didn't exist. Now…here she is. You're embracing your flaws and mistakes. You're owning them, but you're not letting them dominate your life. You're no longer silencing yourself."

I think about that for a second. She's right. Of course she's right. I have been silencing myself for way too long. I've been living trapped in my own fears and insecurities instead of simply embracing myself for who I am. The ironic thing is that the more I seem to embrace myself and my insecurities, the less insecurities I seem to have. It's as if I have only been manifesting them as a way to protect myself, when in reality, they've been hurting me more than they have been helping me.

29

Spring break couldn't come soon enough. I am going back home to California. I am going to spend the week watching beautiful sunsets over the green valley below my parents' house, swinging in the hammock on our wraparound deck, and eating oranges straight from my mom's carefully maintained orange tree.

By the time my mom picks me up from the airport and we finish eating dinner in front of their new wall of windows looking out onto the valley spotted with wildflowers, I forget all about my life in New York. It's as if absolutely no time has passed. I feel like I had never left at all.

"So, tell us everything that has been going on," my mom announces.

We talk every day and I keep her up to date on my everyday life, but she still demands an update as if we haven't seen each other in ages.

"Nothing." I shrug. "Just school stuff. Lots of papers. Midterms. Didn't do very well on my Victorian Literature midterm, unfortunately."

"Like an A-?" my dad jokes.

"No." I shake my head. "Like a C."

"Oh, wow," my mom says. "Well, that's good."

"What?" I gasp.

"It'll build character. I don't think you've ever gotten a C before and this is good for you. To know that you are capable of making mistakes. That you're not such a know-it-all."

She's joking of course. Trying to make me feel better. I appreciate it. My mom can always be counted on for that. She doesn't take things too seriously. At least, not anything that shouldn't be taken seriously. In fact, she always has a way of putting life in perspective. "Don't sweat the small stuff" is pretty much her motto.

That's precisely why I feel so terrible about keeping the events of the last month or so secret. I should tell her. She probably won't freak out. At least, I hope not. Honestly, I have no idea how she would react, but I can't. I'm scared. So, for now, all my mom knows is that Hudson and I broke up. Again. This time for good. So instead of telling her what's really going on, I focus on my grades and school.

"I did a speech for Public Speaking last week," I say. "And it actually went okay."

"Oh, I knew you'd do great!" my mom says,

Still not into you

clinking her glass to mine. We're drinking her specialty—sangria. She makes amazing sangria.

"You know, you can't get sangria anywhere in New York," I say wistfully. "I guess it doesn't fit the climate; it's all gray skies and bleakness over there now, but I honestly think that a little sangria would do New York some good."

My mom flashes her pearly whites.

"Speaking of gray," she says, "you're looking a little gray."

I look down at myself as if I can see my face. "I know," I say with a shrug, "but I haven't seen the sun in close to a month. Honestly, it gets really depressing sometimes. More like all the time, actually."

"Oh, I'm sorry." My mom pats my hand.

Unlike me, my mom looks radiant. Both of my parents are doctors, but they're not working as many hours as they used to anymore and now it looks like they're glowing. Gone are the dark circles and the tired eyes. Their skin looks sun-kissed and they're as fit as ever—given their daily tennis matches at the Calabasas Country Club.

"So, how's the business going?" I ask.

My parents started a clinical research organization, which runs pharmaceutical trials. It took a few years for it to get off the ground, but now they have more time and more than we've ever had.

"Really, really good." My mom smiles. "I'm so glad I'm not killing myself at the hospital anymore.

Now, I actually have time to do my makeup every day and get my hair done every week. Can you believe that? Me actually taking care of myself?"

"I'm so happy for you," I say.

I mean it. They've been working so hard for as long as I can remember, missing my sisters' and my games, events, and special occasions. Now, everything is finally falling into place. They have time for themselves. Time for each other.

"So, okay," I say, taking a deep breath, "there is something I've been meaning to talk to you two about."

"Wait, wait," my dad says and pours himself another glass of wine. My mom laughs.

"You ready?" I ask. He takes a sip and nods.

"Okay, so…I've been thinking about something." I don't know how to say it without actually just coming out and saying it. I look at my parents. They are waiting for the news patiently but eagerly. "I've been thinking of transferring to USC next year."

The table gets so quiet, I hear the hummingbirds flapping their wings as they angle for some syrup out of the feeder.

"Oh, wow, that's a surprise," my dad finally says.

"We thought that you loved Columbia," my mom says. I know she's serious because she puts her glass of sangria down and leans closer to me.

"I did. I mean, I do. It's just tough, you know. Winter. All that darkness and the cold."

Still not into you

"Well, spring is coming," my mom says.

"Hey, if she wants to go to USC, that's awesome. Why are you trying to talk her out of it?" my dad asks.

"It's not that. I'm just confused. I thought you loved New York. This is the first I'm hearing about how you don't."

"It's not that. It's not just New York. I mean, it is, but it isn't," I say. I'm grasping at straws. The truth is that I don't know what it is. I just don't want to be there anymore. I don't want to deal with the cold and all of the bad choices that I made there, but I can't really come out and say that. Any of it.

"Well, I don't know about your mom," my dad says, "but I, for one, would love to have you close by. You can visit on weekends. Go surfing anytime."

I smile. That sounds…amazing. Exactly what I want.

After my dad goes inside to answer a few emails, my mom stays out with me on the deck.

She takes a sip of her sangria and taps her manicured nails on the table. I'm well familiar with this nervous habit of hers. Except this time, something jingles along with it. I look at her wrist. She's wearing a white gold Tiffany's bracelet.

"Is that new?" I ask, even though I know it is. Why did it have to be from Tiffany's? It reminds me of everything I want to forget back in New York. I can't bear to look at it.

219

"Yes," she says. "Your dad got it for me for our anniversary."

"Wow, really?" I ask. My dad has a lot of good qualities, but buying jewelry isn't one of them.

"Yes, and I didn't even have to pick it out myself. He just went out and bought it. All on his own."

"Oh my God," I whisper.

"I know," she says with a laugh. "I thought that maybe he'd had a stroke."

I smile. It's nice to know that no matter how old I or my parents get, they always have the ability to surprise me. I think that's important in life—the ability to surprise others.

I look at my phone. The high of being home is wearing off and I'm starting to feel more and more tired with every minute that passes.

"I think I'm going to go lie down for a bit," I say. "I'm really tired from the flight."

"Okay." My mom nods. "But before you go, Alice, can I ask you something?"

I sigh and sit back down. It's about USC. I know it. I look into her deep blue eyes and wait.

"I know your dad is overjoyed about you transferring to USC," my mom begins, "and I am, too. Don't get me wrong. I'd love to have you close by. We can go shopping and out to lunch. It would be really fun. I miss those Saturdays we used to have together when you were in high school."

"I miss those, too," I say. Suddenly, thinking back to them, I feel like I'm going to cry.

Still not into you

"The thing is that I don't really understand why you're doing this. Maybe that's not my place. Maybe you don't want to tell me, and that's okay, but I just want you to really think about this. I don't want you doing this because things aren't working out for you in New York. Certain problems you can't just run away from. It's strange and hard to believe, but for some reason, they tend to follow you around. Even across three thousand miles."

"I know," I say, nodding. Though I don't really know if I agree with her.

"It's not just certain problems. It's really all problems. What I'm trying to say...rather ineloquently, I guess, is that I want you to come back here for the right reasons."

I nod. I've heard that before, that you can't fix your problems just by changing geography. Changing geography would change a lot of aspects of my life. For one, I would not be living near Dylan anymore—my soon to be ex-husband. I wouldn't be living in the same space as Hudson anymore—the love of my life, up until now, the guy who broke my heart, and the guy whose best friend I married. Oh, what a mess. I promised myself that I wouldn't think about this anymore. None of it. At least while I'm in LA. I've only been here for a few hours and I've already broken that promise ten times.

30

I've spent my week in Southern California walking along the sand in Malibu, hiking in the Santa Monica Mountains, and eating outside multiple times a day. I think that's probably what I've missed most about California. Eating outside is an important part of the culture here. Almost all restaurants and coffee shops have outside areas to eat. Some have simple awnings. Others have elaborate tables, closed off porches, and heating lamps. There's no shortage of them in the Commons area near my parents' home.

There's something magical about eating outside under the bright blue sky and the sunlight. The food tastes different, too. Everything has more flavor. Every kernel is somehow more delicious. Over the last few weeks, I've been stuffing myself with every greasy thing that came my way. Oily French fries. Hamburgers glistening in fat. Pizza with different types of shiny cheese. There is something about the bleakness and the darkness of New York at this time of year that made me want to eat every unhealthy thing that any vendor or restaurant within walking distance of my dorm would offer. So I gorged myself, all in an effort to make the darkness go away. Of course, I was unsuccessful.

Here, under the high sky, which is so high that it looks like not even a rocket could reach it, I suddenly feel free. I don't want grease or fat or oil. No, now I crave something healthy. Something green, definitely organic, and absolutely refreshing. Looking back on the week, the only things I seemed to have eaten all week are fruits and vegetables in a million different ways—smoothies, salads, fresh from the little containers from the farmers market. Just this morning, I had one of my mom's famous green smoothies, which taste amazing by the way, and five juicy strawberries as big as my palm.

"Are you sure these are organic?" I ask. My mom is a stickler for organic produce. She would be horrified to know what I've been living on for the last two months. My mom believes that the body is like a machine. So, in order to have a healthy mind and body, you have to power it on healthy foods.

"Yes, of course. Why?" she asks, taking a big bite.

She's splurging today, apparently. She made homemade whipped cream—something she never does when my sisters and I aren't home—and we

Still not into you

are covering each strawberry that we stuff into our mouths with a generous amount of it.

"I don't know," I say, laughing. "These strawberries are just so huge. I thought that they just had to be zapped with something."

"Well, I got them from Clara at the farmers market on Saturday. She has the most delicious berries."

"Oh, you're just saying that because she's young and is a farmer and you admire anyone who can grow their food."

"Of course I do! In today's day and age, what's more miraculous and uncommon than that?"

I smile, taking another bite. The whipped cream melts in my mouth and cuts the tartness of the strawberry perfectly.

"I can't believe you're leaving already," my mom says wistfully. "I miss you already."

"I know. The week just flew by, but I'll be back in two months. For good."

"For good?" my mom asks.

I think about that for a second.

"Well, I meant the summer," I say.

"And then?" she asks. "Have you given some thought to what I'd said?"

"Yes." I nod. "Honestly, I don't know. I don't really have a good reason for leaving New York except that I want to, but I'm not completely decided yet."

My mom smiles and tosses her hair. She has

such an easy and effervescent quality to her. She's absolutely gorgeous, but it looks like she doesn't even know it. I just hope that in the future, I'm half the put together and confident woman that she is. In fact, it would help a lot if I were that woman already. Then I'd have a lot fewer problems, that's for sure.

My flight is in a few hours and I go to my room to pack. Wistfully, I put away all the clothes that I don't need back into my closet. It's been wonderful wearing all of these tank tops, light, long sleeved shirts, shorts, and capri pants for the week. I must've changed my outfits three times a day just to take advantage of all the clothes that I could wear here that I can't wear in New York. I put away my flats and flip-flops and drag out the Ugg boots that I'll be traveling in. I've had these Uggs since last year, so they are technically my California Uggs, but in New York, I don't wear them with shorts and spaghetti straps. No, there, these boots are my go-to boots and they're often not even that particularly warm.

After completely depressing myself, I decide to take a shower. I put on some Miley Cyrus. I've decided to quit Adele cold turkey because her lyrics and songs were doing nothing good for improving my mood. I need to listen to happier music, I decided on the plane here. For a whole week, I was happy with Miley and Meghan Trainor. Now that I'm going back somewhere I'm dreading, my heart yearns for Adele.

Still not into you

No, I say to myself silently in the mirror. When you're starting to feel down, that's exactly when you need to avoid the things that only bring on more clouds. I skim through my phone for some other music.

Ah!

"Hips Don't Lie" by Shakira.

An oldie, but a goodie. It's upbeat and fun. Exactly what I need. I turn up the music and climb into the shower.

When I lather up my hair, I hear a knock at the door.

"Yeah?" I yell out over the music.

"Hey, honey? I can't find my phone anywhere," my mom says, opening the door. "Have you seen it?"

"No," I say. My mom is always losing her phone. Honestly, not a week goes by that she doesn't call me on my dad's phone, completely frazzled by the fact that, this time, she had finally done it, lost it for good.

"Well, I can't find it anywhere," she says. "Would you mind if I used yours? I just have to call your dad about something."

"Sure."

My mom leaves and takes my music with her, but the good mood that the beginning of the song put me in doesn't wear off. I close my eyes and let the hot water run over my face and body. Light streams in through the window. I love the way its warm rays feel on my eyelids. When I open eyes, I'm greeted by a curious blue jay investigating me from the windowsill. I want to wave to her, but I don't want to scare her, so instead, I just admire the way her feathers dance in the breeze.

Then, right here and now, as I'm watching the blue jay cock her head from side to side inquisitively, for absolutely no reason, something occurs to me.

Oh. My. God.

Noooooooooo!

I turn off the shower and wrap a towel around myself. I don't secure it well and it falls down right before I reach the door. I have to scramble to get it up over my breasts. My hair is completely soaked and water from it runs down my shoulders. My feet leave little puddles on the hardwood floors.

I look into each bedroom that I pass, looking for my mom. Maybe she didn't see it. Maybe she just called my dad and that was it. Please, please, please let that be it. My heart jumps into my chest and I can't take a full breath. I try to slow down my breathing, breathe through my stomach like I had learned at yoga, but I'm freaking out. Nothing's working. Where the hell is she?

Finally, I get to my parents' bedroom. Unlike all the other doors, the door to this one is closed. I open it quietly, but don't bother knocking. I walk in and see my mother sitting on the edge of the bed, staring at my phone. Her shoulders are slumped. Her hair is dangling lifelessly in her face. She's completely motionless. She looks like she has seen a ghost or found out that her daughter not only got married without telling her, but is also now getting divorced.

Shit.

I know right away that it's too late. She has read my text messages, but I think that maybe she hasn't heard me. So, I try to tiptoe out of the room. *Please, don't hear me. Please, please, please.*

"Alice," my mom says quietly. She has a stern tone in her voice, very much unlike her usual tone.

"Hey," I whisper. My mouth is completely dry. I cough a little.

"What is this?" she asks, turning to face me.

Her back straightens out and her chin flies into the air. She's no longer sad. Now, she's angry.

"What?" I ask. Even though I know exactly what she's looking at. I don't know what it is about me, but I have this tendency to deny when I'm put on the spot.

"These text messages," she says, shaking my phone in her extended hand, "from Dylan."

I shake my head. I don't know what to say.

Of course, I can get angry about her going through my phone and reading my private messages, but something holds me back from going that route. I hate to admit it, but a small part of me is happy that my mom found out. This has been a heavy burden to carry around with me and now it's out.

"Alice?" my mom asks. "Do you care to explain?"

I look away and shrug. She throws my phone on the bed. After crossing her arms, she taps her foot a little, waiting for me to say something. I glance over at the screen.

You've been dragging your feet enough about this. My message is highlighted in green.

Sorry. Dylan's message appears in gray.

That's not good enough. When are we finally going to get a divorce?

It's happening, don't fret!

How can I not? It has been forever since we got married. At first, you promised me an annulment and then that was not possible. Now you've been playing games with this divorce. I want to know when.

I don't know.

. . .

Still not into you

I can only see part of the exchange on the screen, but I know it word for word.

"When did you get married?" my mom asks. "Oh my God, I never thought that I would ask my daughter that question!"

"Mom, it was an accident. I was really drunk. Hudson and I just sort of broke up. I don't even remember it happening, really."

Her blank face tells me that she doesn't quite get it.

So, I start from the beginning. I fill in all the details about every little thing and, close to an hour later, she seems to finally get it.

After listening carefully and intently, my mom takes a deep breath. I'm shaking from the cold—I'm still wearing my towel, after all. So much time has passed that my hair is dry in parts and some of the puddles that I've made walking barefoot on the hardwood floor have dried up.

"I have to go get ready," I say, turning to walk back toward the bathroom. "I have a flight to catch."

My mom nods. She isn't angry or upset anymore. She just looks lost. Despondent. Not quite here.

"Before you do that," she says to me, "regardless of all of this, and how hurt and disappointed I am that you didn't tell me about this, I still want you to remember what I said to you before."

"What do you mean?"

"Well, it's a little clearer why you want to transfer to USC, but before you do that, I want you to think about this for a moment. It seems like transferring will make you leave all of your troubles behind in New York and that by simply getting away from New York, you won't have any of those problems anymore. Yu may very well be right, but the thing about problems is that they tend to haunt us. They tend to follow us around, as if they're on a leash because they're not tied to geographical locations, they're tied to us."

I nod.

"Do you understand what I'm saying, Alice?" my mom asks.

"Yes, I do. I'll think about it."

I mean it. Truly.

31

On the plane back to New York, I'm wedged into the middle seat between an old woman with bright orange nails who looks like she's about to chat me up for the whole flight and a large man who spills over into my seat and doesn't even try to contain himself in his. I quickly put in my earbuds and turn up the music on my phone. I want to zone out. This is going to be a really long flight.

No matter how hard I try to fall asleep, my mind keeps racing. I try a breathing exercise from yoga—breathe in through my nose and breathe out through my mouth. After a few minutes, I'm just as awake as before.

The thing that I keep coming back to is how disappointed my mom looked after I told her what had happened. The flicker and brightness in her eyes seemed to have dimmed. She sighed these big, exasperating breaths and her skin seemed to lose all color in a matter of seconds.

I wanted her to yell at me, curse me out, anything but this. I felt like I had actually physically hurt her and I've never wanted to take something back more than I did that.

Shit. I really messed up. I kick myself over practically every decision I've made this semester. Even getting back with Hudson at the end of last semester now seems like a completely foolish idea. If we had never gotten back together, we'd still be friends. I wouldn't have cared about his busy schedule so much and I might've even started dating someone new. Huh, what an idea.

I haven't given that much thought, but I am young. Not even twenty yet and I've only really been in one serious relationship and a very not-serious marriage. Dylan, Dylan, Dylan. Why is getting a divorce from you so difficult? Why has it been dragging on for this long?

I shake my head to try to clear it, but thoughts that I have no interest in thinking just continue to wash over me like ocean waves. I turn up the music and put on my eye mask. Maybe this will help.

Juliet gets back to the dorm a little bit after me. Unlike me, she didn't opt to go home to Staten Island for spring break. No, she had a proper spring

Still not into you

break, full of drinking and partying in Daytona Beach, Florida. She comes back refreshed, though not very well rested. Her skin has a nice deep glow to it and her hair has streaks of highlights—all evidence of a spring break done right.

"Why are you not tanner?" Juliet asks, showing me her bikini tan lines. "Didn't you spend the week in sunny California?"

"I am a little tan," I say. Unfortunately, I don't have any tan lines to show off. "California is different than Florida. The sun there is very powerful and the air is thin. So, it's hard to get a nice tan as quickly as in Florida."

That's always a surprise to everyone who hears that I'm from California and I'm not the color of an apricot.

"I can only get that tan," I say, pointing to her shoulders, "in the summer when I spend all the days at the beach."

"Well, I say that you had missed out then," she says with a quick smile. "Honestly, it was a blast. I won't lie, I did black out a few times; I'm not completely used to drinking from morning to night, but wow, what a party!"

"I'm glad you had a good time," I say.

She went with a whole group of Columbia spring breakers. She didn't know a soul before she went, but is now probably best friends with every last one of them.

"I've got to say, it's nice to get out there and

meet new people," Juliet says. It seems to me that all she does is meet new people throughout the semester. "It gets a little boring to hang out with the same people all the time."

I stare at her. I'm about to say "thanks" sarcastically, but she quickly adds, "No offense, of course."

"None taken."

"You should really get out there more," Juliet says. That seems to be her solution to every problem. At this point in my life, I sort of think that she might be right. I do need to meet new people. Try to shake things up in my life, but in a good way.

"I will," I say. Then it occurs to me. Maybe this is as good a time as ever to tell her about my plans for next year. She might even approve.

"So, speaking of next year," I start.

"We weren't speaking of next year," she points out.

"Okay, you know what I mean."

"Oh, yeah, about being roommates next year, you mean?" Juliet asks, changing into her pajamas. They are purple and have little coffee pots on them. I'm actually quite jealous of how cute they are. "I'd love that," she says. "When I said that it's nice to meet new people, I didn't mean that I didn't want to be your roommate anymore. You're an awesome roommate. There are lots of people out there that are way more obnoxious than you and I'd hate to end up with one of them."

Still not into you

"Well, thanks," I say sarcastically. "But no, that's not really what I was referring to. Actually, I've been thinking about...something else."

I can't quite find the words to say what I want to say. Maybe it's because I've already disappointed one person today and I don't want to disappoint another. Maybe it's because I don't want to hurt my friend's feelings. Sooner or later, I do have to tell her. Be brave.

"What? What's wrong?"

Juliet gets a concerned look on her face. It's unusual and I feel like I'm actually scaring her. Honestly, I didn't know that Juliet was capable of being scared.

"No, nothing's wrong. I'm just thinking that I might not be here next year."

"What? Are you crazy?" Juliet says as her eyes grow wide.

"I'm just thinking of transferring to USC," I say.

"USC?" She repeats the word as if she doesn't know what it means.

"University of Southern California?" I clarify.

"I know what USC is," she says, spreading her arms out wide. Juliet has a tendency to gesture with her hands and speak with her whole body whenever she's drunk or angry.

"It's just something I've been thinking about for a while. I think I need a change. It's close to home, and, honestly, this weather is killing me. It's making me so freakin' depressed."

"Oh, you're not leaving because of the weather," Juliet says. "Don't lie. You're leaving because of Hudson and Dylan and your stupid marriage."

I sigh. She's right, but not entirely. I do hate the weather. The fall wasn't too bad, but this winter is unbearable. The slush and the darkness and the cold. Everyone on the outside seems angry and disturbed by it, too. It's harder to get a cab. It's impossible to see one smiling face in the subway. It's the very opposite of everything that I love and miss about Southern California.

"It's not just them. It's just something I want to do," I say with a shrug. Another thing I want is for this conversation to be over. Unfortunately, given how much Juliet is pacing around the room, I'm not sure that's going to be possible anytime soon.

"Listen, Alice, you'll get through this. You and Dylan are going to get a divorce soon and everything will go back to normal. Next year, we can live in a completely different dorm, just the two of us, and we never have to see Hudson again or Dylan for that matter, if you don't want to."

"You're right. I know, but I really don't want to be here anymore."

She shakes her head. She tries again. She reminds me of all the fun things we did in the fall and that we can do them again. She says she'll hang

Still not into you

out with me more and won't go out almost every night. She's trying her best to convince me to stay. I admire her for that. I listen patiently and say that I'll think about it, but that's a lie. I'm done thinking. I'm pretty set about this.

"Alice is doing what?" I hear Dylan say outside our room. Juliet went into the kitchen and she held this thing to herself for all of two seconds.

"Alice!" Dylan knocks on the door, but doesn't wait for me to answer. Instead, he just barges in.

"What is this I hear about you wanting to transfer? Are you crazy?"

"No."

Great. Another person to explain this to. I had less explaining to do to my parents.

"But why?" he asks. I go into all the reasons all over again. I feel myself being less exuberant about it all, though. I'm losing patience with all of these people questioning my decision. Then Dylan calls me on it.

"We're your friends, you know, right?" Dylan says. "That's why we don't want you to leave. We love you."

That breaks my heart. Dylan's not one for expressing his feelings well. If at all. He's from Connecticut, after all.

"I'm sorry I've been dragging my feet on this

divorce thing. The truth is that the fact that we're still married makes my dad really angry and I sort of love it. Nothing really fazes him much, and this is really getting under his skin, but I'm going to talk to the family attorney in a few days. I'll take care of it."

Finally, an explanation for all the delays. I'm thankful for it, but I also feel like it's too little too late.

No matter what I say convinces either of them that this is really something I want to do and I'm not just running away from my problems here. I won't admit it out loud, but they're basically right. So, we eventually call it a night after agreeing to disagree.

32

When I meet Tea for lunch the following day, she has a completely different reaction to the news. I'm ready to go into a big explanation about all this yet again, but she just nods and says that she understands. She really catches me off guard. So much so that I don't even know what we're going to talk about for the rest of lunch since I thought we'd talk about this the whole time.

"So, I finished my book," Tea announces after we order.

"What?"

"Remember, the romance one about the girl pretending to be a wealthy guy's fiancée on the cruise?"

"Of course! I can't believe you're done with it already." While I've been head-deep in my own drama, Tea managed to write a whole book. Imagine that!

"I'd love for you to read it," she says.

"Oh my God. Yes, definitely!"

"I can send you an ePub version so you can read it on your phone," she says.

"Perfect!"

Tea has been working on the book since January and it's finally done. I'm awed by her dedication. In addition to her classes and Tanner, she has been working on this project and now it's completed.

"Frankly, I'm really jealous," I say when our food finally arrives. I ordered a tuna salad and she's having a grilled chicken panini.

"What? Why?" she says, laughing.

"Because you went out there and did this awesome thing, while I've been burying my head in the sand and dealing with all of my stupid problems."

"Well, another way to think about it is that you've been out there living life while I've just been writing about someone else's."

"Given how this semester has gone, I really wish I had some fictional drama in my life instead of real drama."

"I know," she says sympathetically. "It's been really tough. I'm sorry. I'm sure that when you look back on all this next year, you'll laugh about it."

I smile. "Probably not next year. Maybe in ten years."

Still not into you

"Okay, in ten years." She smiles.

TEA SENDS me her book that evening and I plan on just reading a chapter or two, but seven hours later, well past my usual bedtime, I finally finish it. Wow. The characters are so vivid; they seem more real than real people. They practically jump from the page. I don't remember the last time I devoured a book like that. It's so different from all the books I've read for English classes. Unlike in the books that I've read before, the romance and the love in this one was real.

The characters weren't just people on the page. When they spoke, I heard them. I saw them. I felt them. Their love is real. The girl, Savannah, acted just like I would, or anyone our age. The guy, Tatum, well, Tatum was definitely a better version of any guy I've met. It's as if all of the best qualities of the guys I know, like Hudson and Dylan, were exaggerated to the ninth degree. Don't get me wrong. He has some bad qualities, too, some insecurities, but nothing that his love can't help him with.

I lie in bed for close to an hour after finishing Tea's book, waiting to fall asleep. Unlike all those other sleepless nights I had, the ones that tore me up inside, the ones during which I spent hours beating myself up for all the things that I shouldn't have said and done and all the things that I should've said and done, this night is different. I actually lie in bed thinking about the book. Imagining Tatum and Savannah's love for each other, their first kiss, their first everything. Unlike all these other books, in this one, Tea didn't shy away from fading to black. She took me everywhere, describing every touch, every feeling, every sensation, and every smell. In the end? I fell in love with Tatum and Savannah and I had to have more.

Why the hell did you write this book?

I text Tea even though it's in the middle of the night. Hopefully, she has her phone off if she's sleeping, but Tea writes back almost immediately.

What? You don't like it?

No, I fucking love it!!!

Oh…ok. So, what's the problem?

What's the problem? The problem is that I can't sleep. I love them. I want more.

More?

More about Tatum and Savannah. Are you writing another one? I can't type fast enough.

Um…I haven't thought about it much.

Well, think about it! I'm going to try to get some sleep now. Not likely though, thanks to your book. Sorry not sorry.

After putting down my phone, I still can't get to sleep. This time my mind doesn't wander. I know what I want. I want what Tatum and Savannah

Still not into you

have. I want their kind of love for me. I want to be in love again. I want to feel butterflies over the possibility of touching someone again. I want to wonder how our first date went, whether it was as amazing for him as it was for me. I want to dance in the rain and kiss in a blizzard. I want to live inside a romance novel, but that's not possible, right? That's not reality, right? Yet, reading that book sounded more like the truth than my real life. How is that?

THREE WEEKS LATER, Dylan comes into the living room where I'm procrastinating on working on my Victorian Lit paper. I should be doing research on it in the library, but instead, I'm looking up something vaguely related to Victorian times on my phone and hoping that I will stumble on a topic to write about that way. So far, no luck. Juliet and Hudson are also in the room. Juliet is painting her nails and Hudson is doing his Macroeconomics problem set. Hudson and I have entered another period of Cold War. We don't talk to each other unless absolutely necessary, but we also don't avoid each other at all costs like we used to. So that's an improvement in my book.

Dylan is wearing a wide grin on his face. He flashes me his pearly whites, which do nothing but remind me that I really need to get my teeth professionally whitened. I'm afraid of dentists and all doctors, for that matter, so I've been avoiding them at all costs.

"What?" I finally ask. He's obviously eager to share some news with the room.

He holds up a thick packet in a manila folder.

"Guess what this is?" he asks.

"Your history paper?" Hudson says jokingly. We all know that Dylan did not do very well on his last history paper. By not very well, I mean that he got a C-. Enough for him to start worrying about passing the class.

"Ha ha, very funny. No," he says, rolling his eyes. "No, these are divorce papers!"

I never thought that I'd be so happy to hear the phrase "divorce papers" in my life.

"Really? Are you sure?" I ask, grabbing the packet out of his hand and scanning the papers. They don't make any sense of course; it's all legalized. All I see are the little stickers by the signature lines.

"Yep, got them from the lawyer this morning. You will be glad to know that this divorce is the most amicable one that my dad's Park Avenue attorney has ever dealt with. He said that the two of us were the most mature clients he's ever had."

"Well, that's nice to hear," I say, "given that this is probably the stupidest thing that either of us has ever done."

"So, all you have to do is sign where those stickers are and we're done. A courier will come

Still not into you

tomorrow to pick them up and take them to the court," Dylan says.

"Great! Does anyone have a pen?" I ask.

I want to get this over with as soon as possible. We look around the room, but there's no pen to be found. Then suddenly, Hudson hands me his.

With all the excitement, I had completely forgotten that he was still in the room. Our eyes meet as he hands me his pen and our fingers touch briefly. In that moment, it feels like he can see through me, completely and entirely. Like he knows everything about me that I ever was and ever will be. The feeling leaves me uneasy and scared.

33

I sign each page as Dylan flips the pages for me. He'd already signed his portion at the lawyer's office. When I sign on the last line, a tremendous weight lifts off my shoulders. I give out a big sigh. Suddenly, I'm 300 pounds lighter.

"We're divorced!" Dylan grabs me by the shoulders, wrapping his arms around me. "Divorced! Let's celebrate."

"Woohoo!" Juliet says. "Finally."

"Who wants a beer?" Dylan asks, getting himself one from the refrigerator.

"Wait, remind me, isn't it alcohol that got you into this mess in the first place?" Juliet asks.

"Oh, whatever, buzz kill." Dylan waves his arm at her dismissively. "Alice?"

I shake my head no.

"I still have some work to do tonight," I say. "And honestly, given how long it took for all of this to happen, I'm going to pass on partying with you for a while."

Dylan is the only one who celebrates our divorce that night, but we all take a rain check. Even for him, it's not much of a party. He has only one beer and disappears into his room. Juliet disappears into our room soon after to get ready for another date.

"Congratulations," Hudson says without looking up from his textbook.

"Oh, thanks," I say.

I wait for him to say something else, but he doesn't. So, I go back to taking a quiz about the decade that I should've grown up in on BuzzFeed.

"I know it wasn't your fault how long all of this was taking," Hudson says. This time he looks straight at me.

"Yeah, I know that."

"Okay. Well, I guess what I wanted to say is that I know that, too."

"Okay, I guess," I say.

I hate the weirdness that exists between us when we're alone. In fact, I can't stand it. I'm about to get up and leave when Hudson stops me.

"So, Kathryn and I aren't together anymore," he says.

"Oh. Okay," I say. I don't really know how to respond to that. It's so out of the blue. "I didn't really know you were dating."

"Yeah, ever since that night…of the party," he says.

Still not into you

That's one way of putting it. Another is since that night when she slept over and you made her coffee in the morning or since that night when she slept over and Dr. Worthington came in and made a huge scene.

"Oh, well, I'm sorry, I guess," I say.

"Don't be. It just didn't work out," he says with a shrug.

"Hudson, why are you telling me this?" I ask.

Are you trying to hurt me? I want to ask, but I don't.

"I don't know," he says. The expression on his face tells me that he's not really trying to hurt me at all. He's just over-sharing for no reason whatsoever.

"Did something happen?" I ask. I don't mean to. I don't care. Actually, I don't want to know, but my mouth gets away from me.

"She cheated on me," he says quietly.

"Oh, I'm sorry."

"But it wasn't working out even before that. We just didn't fit right," Hudson says.

I'm still sitting on the couch and suddenly he gets up and sits down next to me. Very close. So close that I can feel his breath on my face.

"I'm not sure if it will ever be right with anyone else," he says.

"Of course it will," I say, waving my hand.

It sounds like he's just having a moment. He's just throwing himself a pity party, but when I look back at him, and I see the way his eyes refuse to leave mine, I know that I'm wrong. He's serious.

"What I mean is that I kept trying to make myself feel like I did when we were first together. Not just with Kathryn, but with all the others."

"What?" I know I should be focusing on the first thing that he said. The first part of the sentence that's a compliment to me, but instead, all I focus on is the second part.

"All the others?" I ask when he doesn't reply.

"Well, you know." He shrugs. "Just all the other girls that I was with this semester."

"Oh, okay," I say with a gulp.

"Don't worry, we weren't serious. Just girls I met at the bar after work. Very casual," Hudson says. He's clearly not aware of the fact that I'm screaming on the inside. *What girls? You were seeing other girls? How many? Why?*

"Kathryn and I were dating, but we weren't exclusive. I just kept meeting these girls downtown and you know what, at the beginning of the night, I had hope that this was the one that was going to give me butterflies. Like this is the one that will catch my attention, but after a night together, I just felt…flat. Like it was nothing."

I can't stand this anymore.

"Hudson, why are you telling me all this? Are you trying to hurt me?"

"No, not at all. I'm saying it as a compliment."

"What?"

Still not into you

"Yes, very inarticulately, I guess. What I'm really saying is that I keep looking for the same connection that we had and it's just not there. You're one in a million, Alice. Maybe one in a billion."

I take a deep breath. Hudson always had an odd way with words. Just when I think that he's trying to be mean or is being dense on purpose, he goes out there and gives me the biggest compliment ever. I'm mad at him for saying all the rest, but I can't stay mad for long because I don't hear that kind of thing every day.

"Well, thank you, I guess," I say. I turn around to leave, but he stops me again. Seems to be in a talkative mood tonight.

"So, what's up with you?" Hudson asks. "We haven't really spoken in ages."

"Well, I just got divorced," I joke. He smiles. We both laugh about the situation. I figured that it would be years before this happened, but apparently I didn't have to wait that long.

"Actually, there is something I've been meaning to ask you. I have to do this final speech in Public Speaking class. It's going to be in a big auditorium in front of all the sessions of the class. I'm terrified, of course, to say the least."

"So, you want help with the speech?" he asks, his eyes light up.

"No." I shake my head. It hadn't even occurred to me that he would want to help. "I just wanted to invite you to it. I have something important to say and, if I can get it out, I'd like for you to hear it."

"Oh, wow, okay," he says. "Let me know the time and place and I'll try to make it then."

"Try?" I ask.

"I've disappointed you enough this semester. I don't want to make yet another promise I can't keep," he says.

"Okay, fair enough."

"Wow, look at us," Hudson says after a moment. "I guess it is possible to be friends even after all that has happened this semester. Hey, here's a wild idea, want to be roommates again next year?"

I stare at him. It suddenly occurs to me that he doesn't know about my plans for USC. I thought that he would find out eventually, given the rumor mill that Juliet and Dylan usually operate, but I guess this one fell through the cracks.

"What? What's wrong?" Hudson asks me.

"Well, I thought that you knew already, but I'm not going to be here next year."

"What?"

All the color in his face disappears. His lips start to turn an awful blue tint as if he's been swimming in freezing water for an hour.

"I'm thinking about going to USC," I say. Why do I always do that? Use qualifiers where they don't belong. "Well, no, not thinking. I'm going to transfer to USC for next year," I clarify.

"Why?"

Still not into you

"Because…because of a variety of reasons. I just think it's for the best."

"How can you say that? Are you doing this because of what happened between us and you and Dylan? Well, that's all over. It's in the past. Let bygones be bygones. You don't have to go all the way clear across the country because of that."

Hudson rambles on for close to twenty minutes about all the reasons that I shouldn't leave New York City. I listen carefully and nod. I'm afraid that if I actually engage in this discussion, I'll never get to bed tonight. I look at him trying to convince me, fighting for me to stay, and a big portion of me loves it. He's actually passionate and animated about something and not so reserved and calculated. I can see that he cares about me. I can see it in the way that he's fighting for me to stay. I appreciate it, really, but it doesn't change my mind. It's all too little, too late.

34

"So, why did you invite Hudson to your final speech?" Dr. Greyson asks me at our next and final meeting.

The weather has turned from cold to wet, but remains just as gray. It has been drizzling all day today. It feels like each raindrop that falls from the sky sucks me of a little bit of my energy. Dr. Greyson is wearing bright red heels, which complement her bright red lipstick and stands out nicely against the grayness of her suit. Looking at that splash of color gives me a little bit of a boost.

"I'm not sure," I say. "I guess I'm looking for a little closure."

"What is the speech about?" Dr. Greyson asks.

"It's free form. It can be about anything. So, I decided to write something about him. About us. But I don't even know if he'll show up."

"If he doesn't?" she asks.

I think about that for a moment.

"You know what?" I say. "It'll be okay. If he doesn't show up, that's fine. This speech isn't really for him. It's sort of for me."

Dr. Greyson's face explodes in a wide smile.

"I'm very proud of you, Alice. You've come a long way."

"What do you mean?" I ask.

"Well, I don't make it a habit to comment like this," she says, "but since this is our last meeting and you've made plans to go elsewhere next year, I might as well go ahead and tell you."

I take a deep breath and brace myself. Dr. Greyson is not one to offer up compliments easily. In fact, everything with her is all about being a work in progress, but I guess that's what life is, isn't it? A work in progress? You're never done growing or changing and there's always room for improvement until that moment when you're no more. I've never thought about it, but that perspective makes Dr. Greyson quite an optimist about humanity. More of an optimist than I am, probably.

"When you first came here, Alice, I saw a broken, hurt little girl. Someone who was afraid to own her feelings. Someone who was afraid to listen to her heart. Someone who was, to a large extent, not very true to herself. Now, you're a different person altogether. You have grown into yourself. You have gained self-esteem. You believe that you have worth and your feelings have worth. That

Still not into you

makes me very proud, Alice. You've become quite a young woman, my dear."

I smile. I want to jump out of my seat and hug her. Then…I do. I wrap my arms around her shoulders in a warm embrace.

"Oh my." She laughs in surprise and then hugs me back.

"I hate to say it, but I think I'm going to miss you," I say, sitting back down across from her. "Coming here hasn't always been my favorite time of the week, but I think I really learned a lot from you."

"I'm happy to hear that," Dr. Greyson says. "I want you to remember that it's not me that you have learned a lot from in this office. It's through the process of reflection. I don't mean to undermine my own credibility, of course, but it was you who has done all the work. All the work of looking back and examining your feelings and actions."

I nod. She's right, of course. Yet again.

"Well, I'm going to miss you anyway," I say with a shrug.

"And I'll miss you."

I look at the clock. Our last meeting has come to a close.

"I hope that USC ends up being everything you're looking for," she says at the end of our session. "If you ever find yourself in New York City again, don't be a stranger."

Walking back home from Dr. Greyson's office, I

feel like I'm floating on a cloud. My feet don't seem to be connected to the ground. It's an amazing feeling to feel like someone, a stranger, is proud of you. My parents have always told me that they loved me and were proud of me, but now hearing it from a complete stranger, I beam with self-confidence. Dr. Greyson is right. I have made a lot of progress this semester. Everything that has happened has made me a stronger and more self-assured person at the end and that, somehow, made it all worthwhile.

I ARRIVE at the auditorium where I'm supposed to give my speech, early as usual. There's a line of nervous students backstage waiting to go on. The auditorium is filled with five classes of Public Speaking students. There have been two sessions of this particular kind of torture and this is the second one. Everyone backstage has been assigned an earlier time and the rest of the people who are going today are waiting in the audience. I make small talk with some of the others, but we're all focused and not really into it. We're all too focused and too nervous about the speech that we're about to make. I'm the third one up and I look over my flash cards. I've written the speech in big letters with a lot of spacing in the words to make sure that I could see it well when I'm up there. I did not take anything to calm my nerves and I'm jealous of the

Still not into you

two girls and guy behind me who are talking about the anti-anxiety meds that they took to calm theirs.

"I can do this," I whisper to myself. "I can do this. I'm going to be fine."

Finally, it's my turn. Everyone is still clapping for the last person who went up. I didn't hear a word of what he said. I walk out onto the stage and force myself to smile. The lights are blinding and I can't see a soul. Something about this experience feels different than the intimacy of my previous speeches. They were all in a room of about thirty people where I could see every set of eyes. Here, there are no individuals in the room. They're just a sea of people. I take a deep breath and clear my throat quietly. I open the lid of my water bottle so that I don't have to fumble with it during the speech if my mouth runs dry.

"Ladies and gentlemen, I am extremely honored to be here and for this opportunity to speak about my friend, Hudson Hilton. For many years, Hudson and I were very close friends. We did everything together. Played with light sabers in our own third-grade version of Star Wars, played endless games of Release and tag, and slept over at each other's houses until our moms grew concerned that we were getting too close for ten year olds. They had nothing to worry about, of course; we were only kids. Then we turned thirteen. Our feelings for each other grew and, eventually, during our junior year in high school, we started dating.

"Dating in high school can be a complicated thing for many. There are a lot of letdowns and mixed feelings, but Hudson and I never experienced these things. Once we were together, we were together for good. We were best friends and nothing could break us up. Then we got to college. Things were more complicated for us in college. For one thing, we broke up right before we got here and then found out that we were going to be roommates."

I pause for effect at the end of the sentence and let the crowd take that line in. There's a gasp that emanates from them. I smile, turn a flash card, and continue.

"Not the easiest thing to go through, as many of you can imagine. College was a time of change. Both for us individually and for us as a couple. We weren't a couple for a long time, and then we were a couple again. Our togetherness didn't last either. I won't bore you with the details, but I'm sure that many of you either heard me relay some of the more sordid ones in one of my unfortunate speeches in class or at least heard about it."

The crowd laughs. I thought that maybe only a few of them would laugh, the people from my class, but the laughter spreads throughout the room. Juicy rumors do fly rampant.

"Well, anyway," I say with a smile, "what I really want to talk to you about is not really our history, but friendship. In college, friends come so easily. You

Still not into you

meet someone in class, they like the same music as you, they also like to go out on Thursday nights, and you're friends. They come so easily, it's easy to take them for granted. You think that it's no problem; you'll just make more friends, but what my relationship with my friend Hudson taught me is that it's not that easy to make friends. It's way too easy to lose friends. So, to close, I just want to ask you all to look at the people in your own life who you care about and give them value. Don't fight over stupid things, and if you fight, at least forgive easily. Friendships are important because they define who you are. The people you meet here will be the people who will forever know you as a nineteen or twenty-year-old. So, when you're an old fifty-seven-year-old, there will still be people in your life who knew you when you were fun and vibrant and full of life. No offense, of course, to all the fifty-year-olds out there. I hope you know I'm kidding.

"So, in closing, I want to say thank you to my friend, Hudson. No matter what happens to us in the future, you will always be special to me because you're my oldest friend. You knew me even before college. You knew me as a third grader and I knew you. I will always value that. Thank you."

The auditorium explodes in applause. I smile and nod and smile again. I can't believe that I actually did that. I gather my notecards, which are limp with sweat, grab my water bottle, and walk backstage. A warm sensation spreads throughout my whole body. Relief. My heartbeat returns to its normal rhythm.

"You were great," someone tells me.

"Thank you."

"Yeah, that was really good," someone else says. I'm not paying attention to anyone who's talking to me. I'm simply nodding and smiling and walking further backstage toward the exit.

I take a big sip of my water, but I don't stop at one gulp. Suddenly, I'm thirstier than I've ever been and I drink the entire bottle without stopping.

"You were amazing," someone says.

"Thank you," I mumble and walk past him.

"Alice?" the voice says again. It's mildly familiar.

"Yeah?" I turn around and see Hudson.

35

Hudson is standing backstage with his foot propped up on the wall. There are wires and poles all around him, but he's standing so casually that it looks as if he's back in our dorm. His arms are by his sides and his face is tilted slightly toward me.

"You came," I say. Still on a high from my performance and the crowd's response, I throw my arms around him. "Thank you."

For a second, he seems surprised by my exuberance, but then quickly wraps his arms around me, too.

"You were wonderful," Hudson whispers into my ear.

"Thanks," I say when I pull away. "I was super nervous, as you can imagine, but I got through it. I can't believe I got through it."

I'm keenly aware of the fact that I can't stop

smiling. I try to press my lips together, but they just won't budge.

"I can't believe you said all those things," Hudson says.

"Oh, yeah, well…I don't know," I say. I don't really know what to say. "That's how I feel and I just wanted you to know that."

I'm owning my words. I'm being honest to my true feelings. Wow. This is a whole new world. A whole new me.

"Well, thank you," Hudson says. "Thank you for saying those things and thank you for inviting me."

"Sure, anytime," I say jokingly. "Actually, no, not anytime. This is the last time. I'm surprised I didn't have a heart attack leading up to this."

"I thought that, given how well this went, you'd be considering a career in public service. Somewhere where you can make speeches all the time," Hudson jokes.

"Hell no!"

We share an awkward moment of silence. Hudson takes a step closer to me. I look up at him.

"Well, thanks for coming," I say. "I really appreciate it."

"No, thank you for inviting me," he says. "I had no idea that you were going to do a whole speech about me."

"What can I say? You are sort of an important person in my life and I want you to know that I

Still not into you

meant what I said. I'm really grateful for our friendship."

He nods his head, hanging his shoulders. Then he looks up at me. His eyes sparkle in the dim light. Suddenly, the moment changes. We are friends one second and more than that the next. Nothing changes except that I know, I can sense, that he wants to kiss me. I want to kiss him, too. He takes my hand in his and looks carefully at each of my fingers, as if he's seeing them for the very first time. Slowly, he brings them up to his lips and gives me a light peck. I know what's coming next. I want it to happen, but I don't let it.

Instead, I take a step back.

"I have to go," I say. "Thanks for coming again."

I walk back home in a daze. I'm on a high from my speech and from the moment with Hudson. I did not give my speech or invite him to it for that to happen. I pulled away because I don't want to spend the rest of my time here and the summer wondering about the kiss. No, it's time for me to move on. Hudson will be in my life as a friend only. That's enough. That was the whole freakin' point of the speech. So why can't I get him out of my head?

FINALS FINALLY COME TO AN END. It's funny how you wait for this one week each semester, dreading it, hating it, and each day of the week passes ever so slowly. Then it's Friday and you look back and bam! Finals week is over. This time I didn't procrastinate until the last possible minute to study for any of my classes and was able to get a proper night's sleep every night. Unlike Juliet, of course. She stayed up all night for what seemed like three days straight.

"Did you end up getting any sleep at all this week?" I ask her, packing up the disaster that is my desk.

I'm not so much packing up as going through all the junk that has piled up in there and throwing almost all of it out. Why didn't I do this earlier again? Why did I think that I would need to hold on to all of this junk mail? Juliet doesn't keep anything and calls me a hoarder.

"Not really." She shrugs. "A few hours here and there in the afternoon."

"I don't know how you're still functioning," I joke.

"Red Bull, baby! Red Bull and about fifty pots of coffee."

"So, what are your plans for the summer?" I ask.

"Oh my God! I completely forgot to tell you," she says, jumping up and down. Her eyes light up like a Christmas tree.

"I'm going to the Hamptons! Well, not just me. A bunch of people I know are pulling together and getting a place there. It's not cheap, but it's going to be epic!!"

Still not into you

"Oh, wow, that sounds exciting," I say unenthusiastically.

"You're a West Coast girl, so I'm not sure you're quite getting the significance of this. This is *the* Hamptons. The Hamptons are the place to be in the summer. There's like a million parties every day."

"No, I get it. I'm sure you'll have a blast," I say, trying to infuse my voice with more excitement.

"And of course, you *have* to come!"

"What?"

"Yes! Please, c'mon. It won't be the same without you," Juliet pleads. Juliet is an expert in pleading. This is probably the exact same voice she uses to plead for things from her father. Its high pitch makes her sound completely helpless, when in reality, she's the only one in control.

"I don't know." I shrug.

"Okay, promise me that you'll think about it. Especially around July 4th or any week or weekend, really. It doesn't matter; they're all going to be amazing!"

"How long are you going to be there?" I ask.

"Two months," Juliet says. "Most people will be coming and going, but I'm planning on soaking up every second of my Hamptons time."

I turn back to packing. I'm almost done with my desk, which now looks like a shell of its prior self. How many students have sat at this desk before? I wonder. How many papers were written here? How many tests were studied for? How many hours were wasted procrastinating?

"So?" Juliet asks.

She walks over to my bed and plops herself on it. There are piles and stacks of clothes everywhere. I have a tendency to fold things first before figuring out what order I want to stuff them into my bags. I do this mainly because I hate to unpack when I get home and often let my bag just sit there half unpacked in the corner of my room. If I'm not going to unpack, then I need to be able to reach all of my favorite clothes easily.

"Okay, I'll think about it," I say.

"Will you really think about it or are you just saying that to get me off your back? You know you say that a lot when you really have no intention of thinking about anything 'cause your mind is already made up."

"Oh my God." I laugh. "You're such a pest. I'll think about it. Really. I promise."

The Hamptons do sound nice. I've never been to Long Island, but I've seen it in plenty of movies and television shows. Maybe it would be nice to fly back here for a week or so and really let loose. If there's anyone who knows how to have fun, it's definitely Juliet.

"I'll hold you to that," she says, getting off my bed. "I'm really going to miss you, girlie."

I turn to face her. She taps her foot slightly on the floor and doesn't look directly at me.

Still not into you

"I'm going to miss you, too," I say and wrap my arms around her.

"Hey, hey, hey. What's going on here?" Dylan walks into our room through the open door.

"Are you saying your goodbyes already? You're not leaving today, are you?" he asks.

I shake my head without letting go of Juliet. We're still locked in an embrace and when I shake my head, we both move side to side.

"So, what's up with the waterworks?" Dylan asks.

Juliet and I finally let go of each other. There's mist in both of our eyes.

"Well, since you're saying your goodbyes already, I wanted to make sure that you've said your goodbye to your engagement ring," Dylan says, pulling out a small blue box from his pocket. "I'm taking it back to Tiffany's today."

Juliet's eyes light up. "Give that to me," she says.

"You haven't taken it back already?" I ask.

Juliet opens the box and puts the ring on her finger.

"Gorgeous," she whispers. "My future fiancé has his work cut out for him."

I roll my eyes.

"Here, you have to put it on, Alice. One last time," Juliet says.

I shake my head, but she grabs my hand and pushes the ring on my ring finger. The two-carat diamond and the little diamonds around the halo sparkle so bright that they make me want to reach for my sunglasses. I find myself transfixed, unable to look away.

"I have to hand it to you, Dylan," I say. "I'm not sure that I'll ever have a ring this beautiful in my life and I want to thank you for that. Whomever you marry in the future will be one lucky lady."

Dylan's face explodes in a wide, effervescent grin.

"No matter what, I have a feeling that you'll be my favorite wife," he says.

All three of us crack up laughing. Even now, I have a hard time believing that the events of this semester actually took place. Wow, what a ride.

36

A few hours later, I'm pretty much packed up. All the posters and pictures from my side of the room are down and all that's left are little bits of glue and tape that I wasn't able to scrape off. It's definitely a sorry sight. Finals have this odd letdown quality to them. There's all this build up, anxiety, and anticipation and work leading up to them. Then, one moment later, they're over and you find yourself at a loss as to what to do. It's like there was a purpose for you being there and suddenly there isn't. It's already my second semester, but I still haven't found a decent way to cope with this feeling. A huge part of me wants to go to sleep and rest, but my mind keeps racing and my body wants to celebrate. We're all going out later tonight, around ten, but there're still hours until then. I plop down on my bed, pull the covers all around me, and wrap myself around my phone. The Internet is always a good way to kill time.

There's a knock on my door.

"Hey." Hudson stands in the doorway. "Can I come in?"

I just started a game of Candy Crush.

"Sure," I say reluctantly, barely able to pull myself away from the screen.

"You going out tonight?" I ask.

"Yep," he says, nodding.

"Cool."

He doesn't say anything for a moment. Okay, I have to put down the phone. He's waiting for me to pay attention.

"What's up?" I look up at him.

He sits down on the bed next to me. A little too close. I pull the covers over and create a little bit of a barrier between us.

"How did your finals go?" he asks.

"Good." I shrug. "I don't really know. I guess we'll see."

He looks somewhere behind me on the wall. I can tell that he's not really interested in my answer.

"You? How was your Macroeconomics final?" I ask. That's his most difficult class. I really hope that he ends up passing it and not just passing, but succeeding.

"I actually think it went okay," he says. His eyes light up at the thought. "I'm really hoping for an A-. That professor never gives out As."

Still not into you

"Oh, wow, that's great. You see, you were worried."

There's a moment of silence. I wait for him to say something else, but he doesn't.

"Hudson?" I say. His eyes return to mine. "What's up? Did you just come here to talk about finals?"

"No," he says, shaking his head. "Not really."

I wait for him to say something else, but again, he is at a loss for words.

I'm starting to get impatient.

"Hudson, what's going on? Is there something you want to talk about? If not, then please leave me alone so I can waste a few hours playing Candy Crush."

"Okay," he says, taking a deep breath. "I just want to apologize for everything that has happened this semester. I shouldn't have worked so hard and ignored you. I really didn't give our relationship a fair shot. Just looking back to last winter and how much fun we had. I'm not really sure what happened when we got to school, except that I was a dick."

"It's okay," I say. "What happened happened."

"No, see, that's precisely it. It happened because of me. If I hadn't been so busy with work and school and actually spent some time with you. Then maybe…"

"No, I should've been more understanding about your job. It was a good experience, right?"

275

"Yeah, I guess." He shrugs. "I just don't think it was worth losing you over."

"Well…it's okay," I say. "I don't really know what to say."

"I also wanted to apologize for getting confused about us. That was partly because of my crazy schedule. I just felt like I needed to get something off my plate."

"Hudson, it's fine," I say. I sort of hate that he referred to me as the something that he had to get off his plate. "It's all in the past."

"You see, that's the thing. What if I don't want it to be in the past, Alice?"

"What?"

I feel myself losing color in my face as blood drains away somewhere to the lower half of my body.

"Don't look so scared," he jokes.

"What are you talking about?"

"I just want to apologize for everything that has happened this semester because I know it's my fault."

"Well, not exactly," I say with a smile. "You didn't force me to marry Dylan."

"I know." He waves his hand to dismiss the matter. "But I know it wasn't for real. I know you don't love Dylan. I just made a bigger deal out of it than I probably should have."

"No, I don't think so. In fact, I think your response was probably quite appropriate given the circumstances."

We both start laughing. It's too ridiculous not to. A part of me is shocked that we're actually laughing about it so soon. I was sure that it would be years before I could laugh about this. Yet, here we are.

As we laugh, our bodies move closer and closer. I'm not sure how it happens, but suddenly, I find myself right next to his face. I look up at him, surprised. Hudson doesn't look so surprised. His eyes sparkle. He licks his lips. He touches my chin and lifts it up, bringing my lips closer to his.

"Hudson," I whisper.

"Alice."

"What are you doing?" He looks down at my lips and then back to my eyes.

"You know what I'm doing."

"No, we can't," I say, pulling away from him.

"What? Why?"

"Because. Because you know why."

Now, I'm getting angry. Does he really not know why? I look at him. He stares at me, dumbfounded.

"Because I'm going home to LA. and you're going to the Bay Area. We won't see each other for a long time. You're going to be here for school next year and I'm going to go to USC."

"So?" he asks.

"So? I don't want to kiss you and then spend the summer wondering what the hell it means. I want to move on from this, Hudson. I can't keep doing this."

"What if I don't want you to move on?"

"What are you talking about?"

"I want to be with you, Alice. I want to try again."

I look at him. He looks earnest. Set in his decision, but I'm not.

"I'm sorry, I can't," I say, getting out of bed. "I don't think this…this thing between us can work. It's too complicated."

"I love you, Alice."

He walks over to me and puts his hands on my shoulders. A few loose strands of hair fall into his beautiful face. It takes all of the strength I have not to just lean over and kiss him.

"I love you, Alice. Do you love me?"

I don't reply for a moment. I could lie, but I don't.

"Yes, I love you, too."

"So? What more do we need?"

"It's not enough, Hudson. I know the Beatles say that it's all you need, but I need more. At least now."

I walk out of the room as quickly as I can because tears are already flowing down my face. I can't stop them. I don't even try. I just hope that he doesn't catch up to me and see them. Another part of me hopes that he does. I want him to wipe them away and say that no matter what, everything will be okay.

Hudson doesn't follow me. I get to the elevator and ride down to the ground floor. It's May and

Still not into you

New York is in full bloom. The streets are crowded with people in t-shirts and shorts. Everyone seems to be running, bicycling, or walking their dogs. I run down to Riverside Park. I need to be alone, but that's pretty much impossible in this city. All I can ask for is to be somewhere where no one knows me. Strangers here don't make it a policy to comfort strangers.

With tears running down my face, I run until I reach the fence separating me from the Hudson River. I stand here watching the river flow by and let my tears flow with abandon until twilight falls.

37

I don't see Hudson at the bar that night. I keep waiting for him to come by. I have my act all ready to go, but he doesn't show up. Dylan and Juliet are clearly disappointed and somewhat angry at me. They're even upset the following day while I'm stuffing the last of my stuff into the few available spaces that I still have left in my bags.

"You know what I'm not going to miss about you?" Dylan says, lying on the couch. "All the drama that you and Hudson had this year."

"Hey, why is that all on me?" I ask. "It's him, too."

"It's him, too. Except that, while you show up after you two have drama, he doesn't."

"That's on him, too," Juliet says, taking my side.

"Thank you," I say.

I look at my phone. I have to leave for the

airport in less than twenty minutes, but I still haven't seen Hudson.

"Where is he?" I turn to Juliet. "I haven't seen him since last night."

She shrugs.

"Dylan?"

He looks down to the floor. I can see that he's hiding something and that he's sorry about it.

"What?" I ask. "What is it?"

"I think he left already," he says quietly.

"What?"

"He didn't say bye to me!" Juliet explodes and then catches herself. "Or Alice."

"I don't know what to say." Dylan shrugs. "I thought that he had said his goodbyes earlier. I didn't think he would just leave like that, but he left about an hour ago while you two were still at brunch."

I feel tears start to build up in my eyes. Why? Why did he have to do this? I try to blink to make them stop and manage to hold a few back. Juliet gives me a big warm hug. I sob a little into her shoulder.

"Please don't ruin my shirt with your wetness," she jokes.

"I promise," I say, even though I'm pretty sure there's already a clear impression of my wet face on her shirt.

After that, our goodbyes are short. I can't wait to

Still not into you

get out of here. The naked walls and the forlorn looks make me sick to my stomach. Dylan and Juliet help me downstairs with my bags. I give each of them a brief hug and promise to come back soon. Juliet brings the Hamptons up and, again, I promise to think about it. Though at this point, I want to put as many miles between New York and me as soon as possible and never look back. I need to get away from here. Maybe then I can forget about everything that has happened.

I hail a cab. When the cab pulls away from the curb, I finally let all of my tears flow freely down my face. The cab driver looks at me through the mirror and quickly darts his eyes when he sees my tears. Too bad. There's nothing I can do to stop them. They just keep coming and coming. I finally manage to get a hold of myself somewhere near the Bronx. La Guardia Airport is still a bit away.

I take a deep breath. It's okay, I say to myself. If this is what he wanted, then this is what it is. I guess I'll never see him again. At least, not for a really long time. That's fine. I got over him before; I'll get over him again. Thank God, I never did kiss him the other night. Otherwise, this would be unbearable.

As we wait for the light to turn green at one intersection, my sorrow suddenly turns to anger. No, you know what, fuck Hudson. How dare he do this to me? All I said was that I didn't want a relationship with him again and he just leaves?

Without a goodbye? Without even a see ya later? You deserve better than that, Alice. A lot better.

When we finally get to the airport, I get out of the cab with a newfound confidence. My tears have all dried up and I'm forcing myself to look forward to a new chapter in my life. Summer in Southern California. There are worse places to go home to. I'm looking forward to the beach, surfing, drinking too much sangria in some Malibu beachside café, and driving a little too recklessly through the winding Topanga Canyon with the top down. It's going to be fun. You'll see.

After I pay the cab driver, I don't bother to get a cart and instead choose to struggle with four large bags all by myself. The ticket counter isn't far; I can see it from here. I don't need a cart. Then I quickly realize that I do. Otherwise, I have to keep dropping my enormous bags off one by one a few feet away from me and going back for the others. I can't very well leave them entirely by themselves as I get in line out of fear of getting one of them confiscated and examined by the airport police.

As I fumble with my bags during one of these mini-trips on my way to the check-in line, I hear someone say my name.

"Alice."

At first, I think they must be talking to someone else. I'm not expecting to see anyone I know here. So, I ignore the voice and keep making little trips for all of my bags.

Still not into you

"Alice!" the man's voice says louder. "Alice!"

When I finally get all of my bags to the place where the check-in line begins, I am covered in sweat and out of breath. I turn toward the direction where the voice is coming from and see…Hudson.

"Hudson?" I ask cautiously. I am actually so physically and emotionally drained that I don't quite believe my eyes. I am seeing bright spots all over the place; maybe the Hudson before me is also a figment of my imagination.

"Alice," he says again. He's dressed in a casual pair of jeans, a plain t-shirt, and he's holding a bouquet of daffodils—my absolute favorite flowers. His hair falls slightly into his eyes and he pushes it out of the way with his free hand.

"What are you doing here?" I ask.

"These are for you," he says. He hands me the daffodils and I can't help but inhale their sweet scent. They smell of hope and springtime.

"Thank you," I whisper.

"Alice, I've thought a lot about what you said yesterday and I've come to the conclusion that you're wrong."

"I'm wrong?"

"Yes. That happens sometimes, you know," he jokes. "Alice, I want you back. I want to be with you. I love you and love is all we need. What else is there that matters?"

"But how is this going to work?" I say, shrugging

my shoulders. "You're going home to the Bay Area…"

"That's where you're wrong. I'm not," he says. He tilts his head, exposing a mischievous smile.

I stare at him. I have no idea what he means.

"I'm coming back to LA with you. On the same flight as you," he says, holding up his ticket as proof.

I don't believe what he says. I look into his eyes. It feels like minutes pass before anyone speaks again. He gives in first.

"I'm going to live in my parents' old house in Calabasas."

He lived in that house since he was born until his senior year in high school when his parents moved to the Bay Area. It's only fifteen minutes away from my parents' house. It's a place where we made a million memories. It's a place that I will always associate with being his home.

"I thought they had sold it," I say slowly.

"No, they just rented it out. They owned it for so long that they barely had a mortgage on it and you know Calabasas, the prices went through the roof. They're getting a ton of money for it in rent."

I don't know why he's telling me all of these details when all I care about is why he's going back to the LA area.

"Anyway." Hudson catches himself babbling. "You don't care about any of that. The only thing that's important is that the renters just moved out and they were going to put it back on the market,

Still not into you

but I asked them if I could stay there for the summer."

"So, you're coming back home?" I ask. The word "home" feels both strange and familiar in my mouth. I don't mean to say it, but Hudson just smiles at me and gives me a wink.

"Yes, I'm coming back home."

He comes a few steps closer to me.

"That way you don't have to worry about us being apart this summer, Alice. I want to be with you and I want to spend the summer with you. I love you."

I inhale slowly. For some reason, tears start to well up in my eyes.

"I thought that you had left without saying goodbye," I whisper. "I was so mad at you."

One lonely tear rolls down my cheek. Hudson takes me into his arms. He wipes my cheek with his thumb. His touch sends a warm sensation throughout my body.

"I'm sorry," he says. "I'm such a jerk."

"You are," I say. "But I am, too."

Slowly, he bends his neck forward. Our lips are so close together that our breaths intertwine. He smells of mint and lavender.

"I love the way your hair smells," he whispers. "Honey."

I smile. It's my new shampoo.

We stare into each other's eyes. Everyone else in the airport ceases to exist completely. I feel like we're in one of those scenes in the movies where the whole world spins around the couple and the couple stands still.

Then, just when I can't wait any longer, Hudson slowly presses his lips onto mine and the whole world explodes into a wild array of colors.

"So, what do you say?" he asks through the kiss. I pull away from him to look into his eyes.

"About what?" I ask, trying to be coy, but the huge smile on my face is exposing my true feelings.

"Will you take me back, Alice Summers? I find myself unable to live without you."

I make him suffer for a moment, and then say, "Yes."

Hudson grabs me by the waist and spins me round and round. My feet leave the ground and I feel like I'm a bird, flying high above the clouds. When I finally come back to earth, Hudson gives me one more kiss, takes my hand, and we head toward the check-in line.

CHAPTER 38

Two weeks later – Malibu, California

CARRYING TWO SMOOTHIES—MANGO yogurt and green ginger peach—I make my way back from the smoothie truck toward our spot on the beach. The sand feels warm and relaxing under my bare feet. Warm breeze toys with my summer dress, making the skirt fly up and exposing my little yellow polka dot bikini bottoms. The sky is so high it doesn't even come close to touching the cliffs of Santa Monica Mountains above me. There isn't a single cloud in the sky.

The sun is bright and hot and the beach is filled with people on multi-colored blankets. White waves rush toward me, tossing boogie boarders in the surf.

Somewhere in the distance, where the water is blue, I see a lone figure sitting on his surfboard.

Hudson.

A second later, he takes on a wave like an expert, dipping his long green board along the waves. He rides one long wave all the way to the edge of the sand. He walks out of the water, holding his board to one side. His gorgeous tan body glistens in the sun, accentuating each chiseled muscle. A few steps away from me, he tosses his hair, exposing his sparkling eyes.

"Hey, babe," he says, dropping the board and wrapping his wet arm around me. I'm burning up—not just from the summer heat—and the coolness of his body brings me relief.

"Thanks for the smoothie," he says, taking a sip. "It's delicious."

"Anytime."

Hudson takes me into his arms and gives me a big kiss with his incredibly soft lips.

"Mmm, salty," I say after the world around us stops spinning and I finally manage to pull away from him.

After he finishes his smoothie, Hudson puts suntan lotion on my shoulders. His hands are strong and I close my eyes in pleasure. He takes extra care to make sure not to get suntan lotion into my hair.

"You ready?" he asks after I take the last sip of my smoothie.

"For what?"

Still not into you

He pulls my sundress off.

"For what?" I ask again, laughing.

Hudson flashes a smile and winks mischievously. Then, before I know what's going on, he pulls me up to my feet, tosses me into his arms, and carries me into the waves.

Thank you so much for reading STILL NOT INTO YOU!

I hope you enjoyed Alice and Hudson's story.

Can't wait and want to dive into another EPIC romance right away?

One-click Dangerous Engagement Now!

To save my father's life, **I have to marry a cruel man who wants me only as a trophy,** but I'm in love with someone else.

"Enthralling!" "Full of suspense, secrets and lies!" "A must read new series!" - Amazon reviews

One-click Dangerous Engagement Now!

Can't get enough of dangerous love stories? TELL ME TO STOP is FREE for a Limited Time!
Download TELL ME TO STOP Now!

. . .

*I owe him a debt. **The kind money can't repay.*** He wants something else: **me, for one year.**

Download TELL ME TO STOP Now!

Turn the page for an excerpt from Tell me to stop…

TELL ME TO STOP - CHAPTER 1

"What are you doing with that thing?" my roommate, Sydney, asks, walking by my room.

I'm sitting on my bed with my hand wrapped around my knees staring at the envelope that came in the mail a few days ago. My name and address are handwritten in careful capital script and it doesn't have a return address.

I showed it to her when it first arrived and she made fun of me for wanting to actually deposit that *ridiculous* check, her words not mine.

"I was thinking that this person must've dropped it off in our mailbox directly because there's not even a stamp from the post office on this thing," I point out.

Sydney shakes her head and walks out of my sightline for a moment to change into her sweats. When I walk out into our living room, I see her boots neatly put away right next to mine in the foyer. The rain droplets skid off her coat and onto the floor where they make a little puddle, which she quickly cleans up.

I met Sydney Catalano at Wellesley College, but we didn't get really close until our second semester of senior year. She was a double major in biology and chemistry and we met in a required anthropology class that we both put off until we couldn't put it off anymore.

I don't know if it's the case with all biology majors, but Sydney is a very neat and meticulous person who always cleans up after herself, and often after me as well. Though I'm not much of a housekeeper, I take out the garbage and kill spiders to try to be a good roommate.

I pull out last night's Vietnamese takeout from the fridge and warm it up on the stove. We each pile as much as we want onto the plates, leaving the rest on the skillet, before sitting down to eat together around the kitchen island.

"So…what are you going to do?" she asks, tying up her silky black hair in a loose bun while inhaling her food.

My eyes meander over to the envelope, lying flat in between our two plates. Sydney reaches over her food and pulls out the check.

"Olive, this is a joke, okay? This isn't real," she says with a full mouth.

I stare at the numbers in the square box. They

are written in the same block script as my address on the envelope.

$167,699.

The amount is written out right under my name and signed with an illegible signature. There is no identifying information anywhere else on the check to give me a glimpse into who it might be from.

"But what if it is?" I ask.

"Why would someone send you a check for this amount and not say who it is or why they're giving you this money?" she asks.

I shrug my shoulders. Of course, I don't have an answer.

"The thing is… I looked up the total amount of my student loans today at work," I say, taking a sip of my water.

"Okay." Sydney nods.

I put down my fork and turn my body toward her.

"What?" She rolls her eyes. "C'mon, the suspense is killing me."

I shake my head. "No, never mind. It doesn't matter," I say, getting up.

She pleads for me to go on and explain but I just take my plate to the sink and wash it. If she thinks that this whole thing is a joke then I don't have to tell her a thing.

"Olive, I'm sorry." Sydney puts her hand on my shoulder. "I don't mean to *not* be supportive. I just don't want you to get hurt. Or in trouble."

I hold up the check to her face.

"You see this number?" I ask, pointing to the amount. She nods. "This is the exact amount that I owe. Down to the penny."

The words surprise her. She exhales slowly and takes a step away from me.

"Really?" she whispers under her breath, taking the check and looking at it more closely.

I nod.

"I had to make a payment today so I looked up the amount, just for the hell of it. Just to make myself feel a little worse about everything," I joke. "But then, the total looked familiar. I realized that I'd seen these numbers somewhere before. I just wasn't sure where. Then when I got home, I saw the envelope on my desk and…there it was. The *exact* amount that I owe in student loans."

Sydney sits back down, stunned by my revelation. I've had about an hour to process this but I'm no less astonished.

"The check arrived a few days ago. So, after you make this payment, you'll owe a little less, right?"

I nod, not sure as to where she is going with this.

"Most of it is going to interest, but yeah, I guess it will be a little less. But the check arrived before this payment was officially due. So, when it came, this is the exact amount of my debt."

We spend the evening talking about the possibilities of what I should do, which basically boil down into two camps.

Still not into you

One, I tear up the check and forget all about it.

Two, I deposit the money, or at least try to.

There is the very real possibility that the check is a fake or some sort of fraud, though whom it is defrauding I have no idea. Still, depositing it is definitely a risk.

"There's something else you should consider," Sydney says. "What happens if you deposit the check and it is real?"

Can't wait to read more? **One-click TELL ME TO STOP now!**

Sign up for my **newsletter** to find out when I have new books!

You can also join my Facebook group, **Charlotte Byrd's Reader Club**, for exclusive giveaways and sneak peaks of future books.

I appreciate you sharing my books and telling your friends about them. Reviews help readers find my books! Please leave a review on your favorite site.

CONNECT WITH CHARLOTTE BYRD

Sign up for my **newsletter** to find out when I have new books!

You can also join my Facebook group, **Charlotte Byrd's Reader Club**, for exclusive giveaways and sneak peaks of future books.

I appreciate you sharing my books and telling your friends about them. Reviews help readers find my books! Please leave a review on your favorite site.

Sign up for my newsletter: https://www.subscribepage.com/byrdVIPList

Join my Facebook Group: https://www.facebook.com/groups/276340079439433/

Bonus Points: Follow me on BookBub and Goodreads!

ABOUT CHARLOTTE BYRD

Charlotte Byrd is the bestselling author of romantic suspense novels. She has sold over 600,000 books and has been translated into five languages.

She lives near Palm Springs, California with her husband, son, and a toy Australian Shepherd. Charlotte is addicted to books and Netflix and she loves hot weather and crystal blue water.

Write her here:
charlotte@charlotte-byrd.com
Check out her books here:
www.charlotte-byrd.com
Connect with her here:
www.facebook.com/charlottebyrdbooks
www.instagram.com/charlottebyrdbooks
www.twitter.com/byrdauthor

Want to hear about new releases, free books and get exclusive giveaways?

Sign up for my newsletter!

YOU ARE INVITED
Want to hear about new releases, free books and get exclusive giveaways?
Join my Facebook Group!

Sign up for my newsletter: https://www.subscribepage.com/byrdVIPList

Join my Facebook Group: https://www.facebook.com/groups/276340079439433/

Bonus Points: Follow me on BookBub and Goodreads!

facebook.com/charlottebyrdbooks

twitter.com/byrdauthor

instagram.com/charlottebyrdbooks

bookbub.com/profile/charlotte-byrd

ALSO BY CHARLOTTE BYRD

All books are available at ALL major retailers! If you can't find it, please email me at charlotte@charlotte-byrd.com

Wedlocked Trilogy
Dangerous Engagement
Lethal Wedding
Fatal Wedding

Not into you Duet
Not into you
Still not into you

Tell me Series
Tell Me to Stop
Tell Me to Go
Tell Me to Stay
Tell Me to Run

Tell Me to Fight
Tell Me to Lie

Tangled Series
Tangled up in Ice
Tangled up in Pain
Tangled up in Lace
Tangled up in Hate
Tangled up in Love

Black Series
Black Edge
Black Rules
Black Bounds
Black Contract
Black Limit

Lavish Trilogy
Lavish Lies
Lavish Betrayal
Lavish Obsession

Standalone Novels
Debt
Offer
Unknown
Dressing Mr. Dalton

Made in the USA
Columbia, SC
26 May 2024